BLACK LACE AND PROMISES

VOLUME 4

FENELLA ASHWORTH

A NOTE FROM THE AUTHOR

T his book contains sex scenes. Plenty of them. So if that is likely to upset you, this is probably not the book for you. It might be better to part company now, before my overactive imagination offends you.

But, to the rest of you, welcome!

I'm delighted you have selected this book to read and I really hope you enjoy it. I am a self-published author who has paused her day job, in order to try and compete in the marketplace with the big publishers. Not an easy feat! The one thing that makes a big difference is to gain reviews from readers, so please do consider leaving a review at the end?

Thanks so much, Fenella x

SOME ADDITIONAL BORING STUFF:

This book is a work of fiction. Names, characters, places, and incidents are either products of the author's imagination or are used fictiously. Any resemblance to actual people, living or dead, is entirely coincidental. If you think you recognise one of the characters in this book then congratulations - your friends and family are *waaaaay* more exciting than mine. Please introduce me some time!

Please note the spelling throughout is British English.

Thank you for your support.

www.fenellaashworth.com

ALSO BY FENELLA ASHWORTH

All books are available on Amazon and KU. Most also have paperback and large print versions. There are also a handful of audiobooks available.

www.fenellaashworth.com

DANIEL LAWSON SERIES

A linked series, charting the life of British equestrian Daniel Lawson and his friends

First Love, Second Chance (Book 1)

Perfect Stranger, Strangely Perfect (Book 2)

Feels Just Like Starting Over (Book 3)

No Rain, No Flowers (Book 4)

Easy Come, Easy Go (Book 5)

Darkest Night, Brightest Stars (Book 6)

The Early Years (Book 7)

Various compilations are also available

THE CRANWORTH CHRONICLES

A linked series based on an arranged marriage with a twist!

To Love, Honour and Oh Pay - Book 1

To Love, Honour and Oh Pay - Book 2

To Love, Honour and Oh Pay - Book 3

ENGLISH BAD BOYS SERIES

Standalone reads where the wicked desires of sexually dominant men take centre stage

Fictional Fantasies Exxxtended

One Hot Wynter's Night

Right Hand Man

REVERSE HAREM - #WHYCHOOSE

Standalone reverse harem reads, containing several men and one lucky woman

Three Times Moor Pleasure

The sequel to this book will be published in 2022

SUGAR & SPICE SERIES

Standalone reads stories of confident alpha men and inexperienced women

Educating Daisy

Patients is a Virtue

Just Another Winter's Tale

FORBIDDEN DESIRES

Standalone reads where forbidden relationships inevitably develop

Management Skills

An Accidental Affair?

Virtually Lovers

Bad Boys go to Heaven

VILLAGE AFFAIRS

A linked series based on the residents of an English village which is far from sleepy

A Very Rural Affair – Book 1

A Very Rural Affair – Book 2

A Very Rural Affair - Book 3

SHORT STORY COMPILATIONS

Black Lace & Promises – Volume 1

Black Lace & Promises – Volume 2

Black Lace & Promises – Volume 3

Black Lace & Promises - Volume 4

Time for a Quick One?

RESISTANCE IS FUTILE SERIES

Standalone reads where powerful attraction leaves the couple ultimately unable to resist

Animal Attraction

Better Fate Than Never

I Put a Spell on You

Highland Games

The Entire 'Resistance is Futile' Series

CANIS HALL SERIES

Wolf Moon (Book 1)

Hunger Moon (Book 2)

Milk Moon (Book 3)

Pink Moon (Book 4)

Flower Moon (Book 5)

Honey Moon (Book 6)

Experimental Pleasures

SMUT ONLY

Written under the pen name Olivia Harding, these are sets of short stories which are heavy on the smut and lighter on the plot!

Don't Stop Daddy Series

Criminally Sexy Cops Series

ROMANCE ONLY

Written under the pen name Sarah Fennel. Unlike all the other books listed, these have no explicit sex scenes

Difficult to Reach

Difficult to Leave

Just Jump!

Walking Out

Trot On!

WHAT'S INCLUDED?

This eBook contains the following three shorter stories:

1) Seven Wishes
2) Our Time
3) Apology Not Accepted

SEVEN WISHES

Sexy racing driver Bradley Drake seems to have it all; ample money, sleek cars, public adoration and a beautiful actress on his arm. That is until a car accident crushes his body along with his dreams.

In comparison, with her beaten-up old van and boringly normal life, Clara Collins is proud to be ordinary. Exceptional at her job as a live-in nurse, it isn't long before Clara proves that she is unlike any other woman Brad has ever met.

On paper, they are two people who couldn't be more different. But when exceptional circumstances bring them together, could Brad and Clara discover what they were each missing, within the other?

Our Time

Annie gets the shock of her life when her son's new Geography teacher turns out to be none other than her own high school crush from twenty years ago. Despite their obvious attraction, Annie and Jack failed to get together back then. But can this chance meeting reignite the secret flame which still burns so strongly between them?

Apology Not Accepted

Carrie is a strong-willed, independent woman who isn't afraid to stand up for herself; character traits which occasionally get her into trouble. Following a misunderstanding with the delectable Richard, she finds herself needing to offer up an apology. To her astonishment, it's an apology that, for his own wicked reasons, Richard refuses to accept. But it doesn't take long for their intensely strong attraction to override any initial playful animosity, and that's when the fireworks really begin.

SEVEN WISHES

FENELLA ASHWORTH

CHAPTER 1

CLARA

It feels a little like an out of body experience as I drive my tatty old van between the electric gates and towards an immaculately maintained property. Trying my best not to gawp, I park at the end of a row of shiny cars, kill the engine and take a swig from my water bottle, in an attempt to moisten my parched throat. Famous actress, Henrietta Glover, lives here. She regularly appears on those ridiculous 'Sexiest 100 women in the world' lists; typically only ever ranked in the low nineties but, let's face it, that's still an achievement of sorts. She's one of the most talked about stars in the country right now and here I am, little old me, turning up at her house for a job interview. I don't doubt that my last client, Joan, was hugely influential in helping me to get a foot through this particular gilded front door, although at the time, I'd no idea Joan had such famous friends. But you know what they say, it's not what you know but who you know.

Taking a deep breath, I exhale slowly before exiting my vehicle whom I fondly refer to as Big Bertha. Looking as confident as I possibly can, I stride towards the huge mansion beneath the blazing, midday sun. Surrounded by wide, sweeping lawns and flower beds overflowing with summer blooms, it is a veritable paradise. I'm not sure I'd need a wage if I was to be offered this job; most people would be happy to work here for free. I raise my hand to ring the bell, surprised to discover the door swinging open before I have the chance to make my presence known. For some reason, I'd prepared myself to be met by Henrietta, although that was probably naïve. Instead, I'm confronted by a tall, whippet-like man, with greying hair and a long nose, upon which a pair of wire-framed spectacles are precariously balanced. I'm guessing he's a member of Henrietta's staff; a legal type, if I'm not mistaken.

'Yes?' he enquires, not looking overly friendly.

'Hello. I'm here to interview for the nursing position,' I explain, keeping my tone neutral, even though I have an urge to tell him to cheer up.

'Name?'

'Clara Collins.'

'Come,' he orders. This time I can't help but react, my nose scrunching up in surprise at his brusqueness. What does he think I am? A goddamn dog that requires training? If it wasn't for the excessively high wage this job was promising to pay, I may well have already walked. But instead, I wordlessly follow his instruction, marching behind him down a long, cool corridor. We enter a small office which contains a lingering odour of garlic. He closes the door behind us and gestures me towards a chair. It is very upright and uncomfortable, perfectly suiting the demeanour of the man whose headquarters this undoubtedly is.

'Prior to interview, or indeed meeting Ms Glover at all, you are required to sign a non-disclosure agreement. If you please,' he requests, pointing towards a printed document sitting innocuously on the desk beside me. With a sigh, I put down my bag and gather up the pages. This certainly isn't the first example of an NDA I've ever been presented with, but I never quite get used to the turgid legalese that someone – I'm guessing Mr Happy here - has managed to stretch across four pages. Nevertheless, I manage to wade through the document and sign on the dotted line, although if they'd just written "Speak to anybody about what happens in the next hour and we'll sue you. Agreed?", it would have saved us all a great deal of time and brainpower.

'If you'll follow me?' the man requests, leading me back out of his darkened room of horrors and into a well-lit and charming space with pastel yellow walls and beautiful floral curtains. I perch myself on the edge of a silk-upholstered chaise longue, fidgeting slightly while trying to look like I'm not completely out of my depth. Apparently content that I won't be causing any trouble, the man departs, leaving me quite alone.

Glancing out of the window beside me, I'm entranced by the scene. A vast lawn, surrounded by acres of rolling fields, makes it feel as though this is the only residence for miles, which I guess it might well be. To the left is the most amazing swimming pool, complete with a diving board and what looks like a bar. I would happily accept a cocktail now, that's for sure.

But just then, all thoughts of Piña coladas and frozen strawberry daiquiris escape me, as the woman herself breezes into the room. Henrietta is perfect; there is no other word to describe her. Tall, slim and blonde, with perfect hair, perfect teeth and a perfect smile. Every guy wants to fuck her and every woman wants to be her...well, apart from me. I'm just gazing in awe, while hoping that she'll give me a job.

But unlike some celebrities who are forever getting into scrapes, Henrietta seems to be universally adored by the media, although this is probably helped by the fact that she's always getting involved in the next big charity event. And just in case her perfection levels require an additional boost, she clearly lives in the perfect property, and I already know she's engaged to super-hot racing driver, Bradley Drake. In short, Henrietta *is* everything I will never be and she *has* everything that most people can only dream of. Consequently, as I rise to my feet in admiration, I have to make a concerted effort not to resent her too much.

'Hello there. Clara, isn't it?' she enquires in her soft tones which are recognised the world over.

'That's correct,' I confirm, following her lead to sit down. I notice she doesn't attempt to shake my hand, although I'm not sure I entirely blame her. With my sensible shoes and boring trousers, plain blouse and mousy brown hair scraped back, the two of us are as different as chalk and cheese. That is, if the chalk is a grubby bit of rock collected from the seaside, and the cheese is of the finest vintage, hand-squished from the udders of an unsuspecting goat.

'Would you like a cup of tea, Clara?' she enquires.

'Um no, I'm fine, thanks.' I get the impression she's expecting me to refuse, so that's what I do. Somehow, I can't quite envisage her making me a cup of tea, and I don't want a maid to have to be summoned, simply for a drink I don't really require.

'Fine, well. Thank you for taking the time to meet with me. You've been highly recommended by Lady Henley, who has nothing but praise for you.'

I nod. I'm not surprised. Joan is a treasure who always sees the best in people.

'So, let's get straight to it. I require a full-time, live-in nurse.'

In my line of work, I always try not to speculate as to who my services might be required for, but in this case, I'm on tenterhooks. My mind instantly goes to Henrietta's family. Given she's only in her late twenties, the requirement could be to help an elderly grandparent, or even great grandparent. I suppose it could be a parent having been taken sick, although I've heard nothing in the news and I did do my research thoroughly before accepting the interview. Believe me, every aspect of this woman's life is chronicled, from the green gunky kale smoothie she had for breakfast, right down to the earrings she chose to wear to a certain party. Or maybe only the best parts of her life that she wants to share are actually made public…I don't know.

'Certainly,' I confirm. After all, that is my job. It's not a glamorous one and it never will be, but I'm good at it. 'Will the successful applicant be required to live here?'

'No, not to live here. At another residence about twenty miles away.'

I nod again. That would suit me perfectly, being close enough to enable me to visit my own precious family during any down time.

'And may I ask who the care is required for?'

'You've signed the NDA, right Clara?' she enquires, her eyes narrowing.

Her question is rather superfluous in my opinion and I suppress a huff of exasperation. I can't imagine I'd be permitted access to this room by Mr Happy otherwise. But regardless, I play along.

'Yes, I have.'

'And you understand the consequences of breaking that, Clara?'

For a moment we stare at each other. Perhaps this woman isn't quite so perfect after all because I'm finding her increasingly annoying. Particularly her continued use of my first name in conversation. It's almost as though she's congratulating herself for remembering it.

'I understand the consequences,' I confirm. 'And please let me set your mind at rest. I've worked under NDA's for over fifteen years and, if you look into my background, you'll discover they have never been broken. For some of the families I've worked for, discretion is almost as important as skill in my line of work, so please let me give you my word that I will not share anything I witness or hear with anybody.'

'Very well,' nods Henrietta. 'In that case, the care is required for Bradley... Bradley Drake.'

Well, there were any number of scenarios which had been rattling around my imagination, but it's fair to say that wasn't one of them.

'Your fiancé?' I say stupidly, receiving only a tight smile in return. 'I hadn't heard.'

'And that's exactly how we intend to keep it. A secret. Understood?'

'Of course. May I ask about the extent of care he requires?'

'He had an accident a few weeks ago and his injuries are significant. Along with a multitude of broken bones, he's suffering from soft tissue damage too.'

'Poor man,' I breathe, aware of the months of physio which will be ahead of him.

'Mmmm,' she agrees. 'The prognosis isn't good that he'll ever fully recover. And he'll certainly need full time assistance for the next three months, at a minimum.'

I study her curiously. Broken bones and soft tissue damage aren't a great deal of fun but, over time, improvement will surely be made.

'I'm sorry to hear that.'

'I like you, Clara,' Henrietta admits, her face cracking into a small smile. 'Given what you know, are you still happy to be interviewed?'

'Oh, er. I was under the impression *this* was the interview?' If I look confused, it's because I am.

'No,' she laughs. It's a light, tinkling affair that I instinctively know would get on my nerves within a relatively short time frame. 'Bradley might be physically broken, but mentally he's as strong as ever. He's insisting on interviewing the successful candidate which I guess is only fair, given he'll be living with them in his house?'

'Of...of course.'

'In that case, please come this way.'

A few minutes later, I'm following Henrietta's black stretch limousine out of her property and back onto the main road, just hoping that rusty, ancient old Bertha doesn't take it upon herself to break down. Without doubt, we are the strangest convoy I have ever witnessed.

CHAPTER 2

BRAD

I keep telling myself things will get better. That's the only way I'm managing to avoid having a complete fucking meltdown. I just hope I'm not lying to myself, because the truth of the matter is, life is shit right now. And I mean *completely* shit. I guess the only positive is that I'm out of hospital at last, but that really is the only positive. After all, I'm still lying on my back in bed, when I'd rather be outside enjoying myself. My dear parents are doing their best but, even with the best will in the world, they can't be expected to put their entire lives on hold for me. Which leaves me with Henrietta's ancient secretary, Mary, filling in, on the rare occasions my parents take a break. Mary was once a nurse in the Falklands war, or so she says. I'm not convinced at all though. Much more likely that she was a fighter pilot than a caring medical professional. Any warm bedside manner is distinctly lacking, that's for sure.

Not that I allow her to do anything other than help me take my pain medication every four hours. Ideally, I wouldn't be taking it at all. It makes me feel nauseous and dizzy for large parts of the day. At first I stubbornly refused to take any medication, but the pain became so excruciating that I was finally forced to relent. I guess given I've got two broken legs, two broken arms, a face and neck which is smashed up, along with concerns about my spine, I shouldn't exactly be surprised. I've always been such a strong-minded, strong-willed and highly capable individual. Now I'm reduced down to a cripple who can't even fulfil his own basic needs, or refuse medication that ideally would be avoided. Like I said: life is shit.

Just then, Mary re-enters the room and temporarily breaks my negatively spiralling thoughts.

'Excuse me, Sir, but Miss Henrietta's at the door.'

'Tell her to bugger off,' I snap back. But apparently Mary is becoming immune to my bad language. This time, she doesn't even flinch. I silently acknowledge that I'll have to up the ante next time, if I'm single-handedly going to maintain that shocked and disapproving look on her face. Instead, she disappears for a minute or so, before returning with a worryingly determined expression.

'Apologies Sir, but Miss Henrietta is insisting. You see, she's brought a full time nurse for you to interview.'

'Fuck's sake,' I huff, seriously not in the mood for any of them right now. I can just imagine what the woman will be like and I don't need her. And I certainly don't require Henrietta to thunder in here, all blonde highlights, long eyelashes and false tits. What the hell I ever saw in that woman, I can't fathom. I guess her beauty blinded me, but I can see straight through it now. My eyes have truly been opened.

'Can you tell them both,' I begin. 'And I want you to use these *exact* words.'

Mary nods at me, no doubt bracing herself for what will follow.

'Tell them to go fuck themselves.'

This time, Mary's mouth all but vanishes at her obvious disapproval of my language. I chuckle to myself as she marches back out of the room. Being cantankerous is the only thrill I get these days. I still have my own voice. It's one of the few things that hasn't been taken away from me yet, and I sure as shit intend to use it. I smirk a little further, as I imagine the scene taking place down the corridor. My pompous once-betrothed stomping off in a temper, followed by some nanny type. I can just see her now; a bossy, middle to late aged, large-breasted monstrosity of a woman, her tweed skirt straining at the seams, put onto this earth solely to make my life a misery. Well, it's just not happening. I've had enough. My parents and I can manage quite adequately.

A few minutes later, I hear a car door slam, followed by the sound of a vehicle driving away. It gives me a perverse thrill, sure in the knowledge that I've won that round. But to my astonishment, the bane of my existence returns to the room shortly afterwards with a message.

'After your rudeness, Miss Henrietta has quite understandably departed,' explains Mary, her expression making it quite clear that she doesn't blame her one iota. 'But the girl who came here to be interviewed says she's quite happy to wait outside until your mood improves.'

'*My* mood?' I roar. Fucking cheek. But against my will, I discover that my interest is piqued. 'What do you mean, *girl*?'

'Well, she's a girl compared with me,' shrugs Mary. 'Shall I let her know that she'll be waiting quite some time before we see any improvement?'

I stare at Mary, astonished by her impertinence. My legs are involuntarily starting to shake again, and I take a deep breath, in the hope that I can still them once more.

'I can assure you there is nothing whatsoever wrong with my mood,' I growl. 'Show her in.' After all, if I do manage to employ a nurse, I can dispense with the unwanted services of Mary, and Henrietta's influence over my life will be further diminished.

A short while later, an attractive woman of about my age steps into the room. She is tentative, but still I observe an underlying confidence there. I have no doubt that she's been prepped about my sharp tongue and general bad temper by Mary. But that isn't who I really am. Not deep down. I'm just dying inside, desperate to be allowed to live again, and sometimes the pain and frustration gets to me. I notice that she has kind eyes and a gentle face, as she smiles at me anxiously. But I don't smile back; as far as I'm concerned, she is still Henrietta's mouthpiece to some extent and until she proves otherwise, I won't make the mistake of trusting her.

'How can I help you?' I ask.

'Um...' She looks confused, as well she might. But my purpose in this situation is not to make this easy for her.

'I've been asked to interview for your live-in carer.'

'Oh yeah?' Again, her nose scrunches up with confusion. I know it's pathetic, but it feels like I haven't had fun in so long. If terrorising visitors is the extent of my entertainment these days, then I'll make the most of every given opportunity. In my younger years, I'd always been so impish and playful...until I met Henrietta of course, when that behaviour was largely squished out of me. But I yearn to be that man again; Trouble, with a capital T.

'Yes...my name is Clara.'

'So tell me, Clara,' I say, briefly taking pity on her. 'Who have you worked for before?'

She reels off an impressive list of people that I'm not entirely sure I believe. Clara seems a little too nice to be working with some of those families, if their reputations are to be believed.

'And what are your key skill sets?' I ask, starting to get into the swing of this interviewing game. Not that I'd ever imagined I would one day be questioning a woman while lying in bed.

'Well, I'm a nurse by profession,' she explains genuinely. 'Over the years, I've learnt to become a fairly decent cook too...after all, eating well is often one of the key roads to recovery.'

'Is that so?' I enquire, questioningly raising my eyebrow as I turn on a little charm.

'Yes,' she stutters, and I'm enchanted to observe that she's actually a little shy in my presence. Not that I can imagine why. Once upon a time, I used to be a good looking guy, but not now. Nobody in their right mind could be attracted to this busted, broken train wreck.

'Well, you seem perfect for the job to me,' I admit, attempting to keep a straight face as my imagination comes up with a daring and rather unexpected suggestion that I just can't resist asking. 'And I only have one more question.'

'Which is?' she asks, continuing to look apprehensive.

'How skilled are you at giving blow jobs?' I physically have to bite the inside of my mouth, to prevent myself from laughing. But like I said, in my current state, I have to get my kicks where I can. I'm astonished to discover my question hasn't made her rush out of the room in disgust. On the contrary, she is staring intently at me with those sparkling brown eyes, refusing to back down.

'I can assure you, Mr Drake. That information is on a strictly need to know basis.'

Excellent. So the kitten has claws after all.

'In that case, I do believe you're hired,' I say. 'That is, if you still want the job?'

'I would love the job, thank you!' she replies, looking genuinely delighted.

'Good. Welcome aboard. I would shake your hand, but that's a bit of an issue right now,' I sigh, nodding towards my arms which will remain in plaster for the next three weeks apparently. Joy. 'Your first duty is to get rid of that fucktard Mary and ensure that both she and Henrietta never set foot in my home again.'

Clara looks confused by my request but doesn't argue, instead walking straight out of the room. She returns five minutes later with a smile on her face.

'Consider them both banished,' she confirms. Secretly, she's already my hero. 'Now, are you up to having a little chat, so I understand exactly what you require me to do?'

'Sure,' I shrug. After all, what the hell else have I got to do, except just lay here and watch the most tedious daytime television shows known to man, while everyone else gets on with their lives around me as before.

'All your medical and nutritional requirements are well documented, so I'll be studying those very shortly. But firstly, I'd like to understand what it is that *you* want.'

I gaze at her stupidly, angry at myself for allowing tears to start building up along the lids of my eyes. I blink quickly to disperse them. Over the past few weeks, I'm not sure anyone has actually asked me what I want. Their focus has been about what the medical profession has told me I need. The meds I'm obliged to take. What the doctor advised should be done. Personal choice has been ripped out of the equation, and now Clara's here attempting to reverse that worrying trend.

'This is only temporary, you know?' she says reassuringly, no doubt in an attempt to fill the growing silence as I struggle to form a verbal response.

'I *beg* your pardon?' I ask incredulously, quick to recover my anger which is always bubbling so close to the surface these days.

'You...feeling like this,' she tries to explain. 'It's natural to feel down following an accident, but I'm given to understand that your injuries are only temporary. You will recover.'

'Well, you're given to understand wrong,' I snap back, not wishing to receive a positive pep-talk, when there is absolutely nothing good about my future. 'And as talented as you might well be at nursing, I'm not even sure *you* can reverse...'

'Reverse what?' she asks cautiously, as my words dry up to nothing.

I know I shouldn't take my anger out on this woman who is only here to help me, not least because I'm pretty sure her lack of understanding stems from Henrietta being typically frugal with the truth, but I can't help it.

'I could require a walking frame for the rest of my life!' I explode, all my frustration directed at Clara. 'I've been told the movement in the lower part of my body might never fully recover. Do you have any idea how that feels? Overnight, I've changed from being a successful man with full control over his mind, body and actions, to this needy, dependent, impotent burden!'

Unsurprisingly, Clara looks taken aback for a moment, but swiftly recovers when my increased levels of stress cause the shaking in my legs to suddenly escalate. I cry out as the agonising cramp sets in. Without pause, Clara approaches me, takes a firm hold of my thighs and starts to manipulate them. I have no idea what she's doing, but it's working. Within seconds, the pain starts to subside and my limbs slowly begin to still.

'You sound like a man who has given up, and that's the only thing

I'm going to be concentrating on reversing,' she explains gently, continuing to massage my legs and helping to allay my fears. 'You have to fight for your recovery, fight for what you want in the world, and that's what I'm here to help you with.'

'I'm not sure even you can undo a medical certainty,' I observe wryly, not really meaning to argue with her, but equally, not being able to stop myself either.

'Perhaps I can't, but that's not what we're talking about here, is it? And even if it is, you still have the ability to move beyond where you are today and improve your life considerably.'

The strange thing is, Clara's welcome, soothing presence and gentle touch is truly making me believe in her. And although I'm never going to admit as much out loud, she's kind of got a point. These last few weeks have been the most miserable of my existence. Never before have I considered ending my own life, but those thoughts have been daring to creep into my mind recently. And although the idea is terrifying, in my darkest hours, it has also been calming; there is a potential way out of this. Her soft voice fortunately breaks my destructive train of thought.

'So, I'll ask you again. If I could give you one wish, what would you want?'

'I'd want to have a beer down the pub with a mate,' I sigh, with almost indecent longing. 'Feel the sun on my face, the sand between my toes and breathe in the salty air, as I enjoy fish and chips by the sea. To wear my own clothes...'

'These aren't your own clothes?' she asks, in genuine confusion.

'Of course they're fucking not!' I exclaim, sending her a disbelieving glance. 'No, these fucking hideous monstrosities were bought for me...because oversized T-shirts and plenty of Velcro apparently make it easier to dress me in my crippled state.'

Clara reacts calmly to my outburst, simply continuing to squeeze my thighs, as my anger sets off another physical tremor.

'Understood. Anything else?'

'I want to enjoy a proper bubble bath, not some fucking hideous, hand-towel, flannel-washing affair that makes me feel less than human.' And yes, I am on a roll now but I don't care. 'To get out of this fucking bed and be seen as a man again and not just a problem to resolve. And possibly most importantly, to stop this goddamn, continuous *fucking* shaking!' Although to give Clara credit, whatever she's doing to my legs right now is helping to provide relief.

'You're well aware that I only offered you one wish, and you've just listed six?' she observes, the hint of a smile creeping across her lips. I shrug unapologetically.

'Fine,' she laughs. 'With the possible exception of drinking beer...I'll have to check your meds... I think we can manage all of those within the next month.'

'Seriously?' She can't mean it?

'Of course. If I'm going to set you the challenge of recovering, then I have to do what I can to make you believe it's worthwhile trying. That you've got a life worth recovering for.'

Little does she know, by just being here, Clara is already doing that.

CHAPTER 3

CLARA

I start work on Brad's bucket list of wishes almost immediately. In my mind, his needs are a priority because providing them will start to give him the confidence and desire to recover. The quickest win is obviously his request that he wears his own clothes and within half an hour, I ensure that wish is granted. I certainly can't blame Brad for wanting that; when times are tough, we all need comfort and familiarity around us. I'm really not sure what his previous carer was thinking, taking that basic requirement away, but the unexpected smile he sends me once he's back in his own T-shirt and shorts brightens up my day considerably. Hell, what am I saying? It brightens up my month! The guy might be my patient, but still he effortlessly oozes sex appeal, even in his damaged state. Sure, dressing him in his own clothes is a little more work for me, but in the long run, it is well worth the effort.

It's true that Brad's remaining five wishes will take a little more planning, but I've never been afraid of a challenge. Besides, the one thing both of us have available right now is plenty of time; time which we funnel into web-based research and chatting through the options. Now that he's relaxed in my company and we've started to build an embryonic trust, I have to admit to really liking him. Despite his injuries, he's a seriously attractive man. But more important than that, he's funny, intelligent, determined, thoughtful and kind. Henrietta is one very lucky woman...speaking of which, I really don't understand what is going on there. She hasn't attempted to make contact since I asked Mary to inform her not to visit, and Brad hasn't enquired after her at all. But it's not really any of my business, so I don't ask questions.

'It definitely needs to be a walk-in bath,' I explain. Under his request, I'm sitting cross-legged beside Brad on his double bed, navigating through the various websites which he's asking to see. A light summer breeze is wafting in through the open window, occasionally distracting my attention.

'That's slightly ironic, given I can't walk,' he huffs. His frustration is understandable but I feel obliged to correct him.

'It's pretty tricky to walk with one broken lower leg and one fractured one,' I observe, arching an eyebrow in his direction. 'Give it time.' But I know what he's alluding to; his accident caused some damage to his spine and although he has feeling and movement in his legs, the extent to which the injury will affect his mobility in the longer term is currently unknown.

'That one, then,' he proposes, nodding towards the top of the screen. 'How long will it take to be delivered?'

'Three to five working days,' I reply, having made a couple of rudimentary clicks on the mousepad.

We've already agreed that the bath will be installed in my bathroom, which is adjoined to my bedroom here. Brad is very fond of his own shower room and has no desire to rip it out in order to make way for something utilitarian and far inferior. I can't say I blame him, even though I wonder when he will next be able to use his own beloved facilities. Given that money is clearly no object, if the luxury of his home is anything to go by, installing new facilities seems the sensible option. And I've already managed to have a chat with my go-to plumber, who also happens to be my uncle. As a favour, he's willing to give up a weekend to install the bath. So with any luck, very soon, I'll be able to help deliver Brad's next wish.

'Can you order it then, please?' he requests. 'My credit card should be in my jacket pocket.'

Carefully, I crawl off the bed to avoid jarring him too much and locate his leather wallet, bringing it back to the bed. It feels very strange to rifle through such a personal item, particularly when the man who owns it is located mere inches away, but under his instruction I place the order.

'Thank you,' he says, exhaling a long sigh. 'It feels as though we've accomplished something.'

'You speak as though you've just completed all of your tasks for the day, when actually the opposite is true,' I observe, beaming at him.

'Huh?'

'You and I are going out now.'

'I'm not mobile enough for that...besides, I don't wish to be recognised.'

A celebrity in his own right well before embarking on a relationship with the fragrant Henrietta, I do understand why Brad doesn't wish to attract attention. So far, the media haven't snapped up the story of his injuries and the last thing I want to do is upset that status quo, but equally, he can't remain boxed up indoors for months on end. Particularly not on such a beautiful day.

'We'll manage,' I argue, adamant that we will take this next step towards his recovery today. 'You are quite mobile enough and trust me when I say, *nobody* seeing my vehicle will expect the great Bradley Christian Drake to be travelling around inside.' Sending him a cheeky wink, I exit the room, the sound of his amused voice ringing in my ears.

'Oh God! I'm not gonna like this, am I?'

'On the contrary,' I reply, sneaking my head back around the door of his bedroom. 'You're going to absolutely *love* it!'

———

'A GENTLEMAN WOULD OPEN the gates in these circumstances,' grumbles Bradley behind me, as I slide back into the driver's seat and pull away. But his grumbling really is half-hearted; I can tell from the change in his posture alone that being outside of the house is doing him the world of good. As promised, I've managed to load him into a wheelchair and then push him into my crappy old van, which is specifically fitted-out for that very purpose. With every window wide open, we are now heading down a private farm track that's owned by a friend of mine. Interspersed with five-bar gates, I have to keep stopping the vehicle, in order to deal with them.

'A gentleman might well open the gates,' I agree, a grin spreading across my features. 'But have you ever *seriously* been described as one of those?' I glance at Brad through the interior mirror and manage to catch his eye, before sending him a wink.

'Bloody cheek!' he chuckles, the corners of his eyes crinkling with amusement. It's the first time I hear him laugh and it unexpectedly causes the hairs on the back of my neck to prickle. Silently, I vow to insult him more regularly, if that glorious sound is the result. 'I didn't agree to join you, just to be insulted and driven around in...this,' he clarifies with mock disgust, already quite aware of how attached I am to Big Bertha.

'Oi!' I complain. 'You wanted incognito, so that's what I've provided!'

'Well, there's certainly no denying this is *incognito*...along with a few other choice phrases I could mention.'

'I will not sit here and listen to you insult Bertha!' I conclude. With a chuckle, I turn up the radio significantly to allow one of my favourite tunes to fill the air. I quickly discover that it's also one of Brad's favourite tunes too, because the two of us are soon singing at the top of our voices as the music blares around us. Only when we reach the isolated cliff edge, a crystal-clear coastline stretching all around us, do I turn off the radio and allow Bertha to rest.

'What's going on? Joint suicide pact?' queries Brad, sounding playful.

Ignoring this comment, I exit the vehicle, lower the back ramp and push his wheelchair out onto the short grass. Noting a perfect location where we can just sit and exist for a while, I start to push Brad in that direction, talking as I do so.

'You know animals don't suffer from PTSD or ongoing stress, don't you?'

'Huh?' he asks in astonishment at this surprising change of subject. 'What are you? A vet now?'

'I do sometimes think I'd get more sense out of animals than human patients,' I reply.

'And a comedian too?' he chuckles, managing to turn enough to glance up at me. The feeling when our eyes lock is most disconcerting. 'Go on then, I'll bite. Well, not literally, unless you want me to?'

Instantly flushing red, I drag my eyes away from his wickedly twinkling ones and focus on the path ahead.

'So, why don't animals get PTSD?' he enquires, thankfully returning the conversation to much safer ground.

'Because they deal with their emotions in the moment. They don't bottle them up for weeks, months, years at a time. They expel them and then they move on.'

We've reached the viewpoint I was aiming for. Gratefully, I stop pushing and apply Brad's wheelchair brakes carefully. The location is very exposed here, the wind blustery, forcing me to raise my voice further to be heard.

'After a nasty incident, an animal will shake dramatically, or verbally shout out their emotions. In comparison, humans bottle stuff up. As children, we're taught to withhold and suppress our feelings, but it can be a really good thing to let your emotions go once in a while.'

'And your point?' enquires Brad. It is said in a genuine way, without his trademark sarcasm, although that might be because he practically has to shout, in order to be heard.

'Part, if not all of the reason your legs go into spasm is because of a build-up of stress. Your body is trying to restore neurological equilibrium itself, because you're crap at doing it naturally.' I smile at Brad's look of disbelief that I've just dared to call him crap. 'So I want you to scream at the sea.'

'Come again?'

'Shout!' I holler, loving the fact that I can raise my voice without repercussions. Knowing that only nature can hear me feels incredibly liberating. Well, nature *and* Brad.

'Fuck!' he bellows, somewhat reluctantly.

'Now that really was rubbish,' I chide. 'Try harder!'

It doesn't take too many more attempts before we are screaming into oblivion, both of our faces red from the exertion, our eyes dancing with glee. Eventually, we become silent and I collapse onto the grass beside Brad, feeling completely high on life. There's no way he can tell me that doesn't feel better. With my eyes closed, I absorb the warmth of the sun, content in the bubble which contains just the two of us.

'Clara.' I hear his tender voice being carried upon the wind. Opening my eyes, I turn to look at him, seeing a range of emotions there that I can't quite decipher.

'Yes,' I nod, kneeling up beside him.

'This has been the most amazing day. Thank you.'

We smile at each other, despite our swirling emotions.

'You're welcome,' I reply. 'But know that I intend to bring you up here every day, wind, rain or snow, until your body stops involuntarily shaking. You have been warned.'

Suddenly, looking at Brad is too intense. It feels dangerous, almost like staring at the sun. So instead, I turn to face the seagulls dive-bombing from the cliff edge towards the sea and enjoy the beauty and relative safety of nature. But Brad is correct. It has been an amazing day. If only every day could feel like this. And if only I could find someone equally as special as this man to share those days with. Although the truth is, I'm pretty sure Bradley Drake is one of a kind.

CHAPTER 4

BRAD

Some weeks have passed since Clara first joined me and I'm honestly struggling to remember life without her. I don't say this lightly, but she has completely changed me, quickly banishing the depressing, hopeless state I was originally in. Certainly, for a while, she was the only bright star on an otherwise very dim horizon. I'm also eternally grateful that she's taken a huge burden off my Mum and Dad. I can see them as parents again now, rather than carers, and our relationship has improved dramatically because of it. We are able to enjoy the fun times, rather than just making it through each day. Pathetically, I do miss Clara when I'm with them, but I appreciate that she needs some down time too. I try not to dissect our situation too much, but in my darker moods, I remember that I am just a job to her. We aren't spending time together for any reason other than she's being paid to be here.

Fortunately, such moments are few and far between now, and today has been another positive day. Clara took me to hospital to have the various plasters removed and undertake my first physio appointment without them. Somehow, she even made that seem fun, although it wasn't nearly as enjoyable as our regular trips out to the farm. As she promised, or should that be threatened, we have enjoyed many trips to scream into the swirling marine wind. Although recently, there has been a lot less screaming and a lot more talking. I am undoubtedly feeling calmer and more content and, as Clara predicted, my body shakes far less as a result. Another one of my wishes has apparently been granted...and another one too. Thanks to my plasters being removed, I'm enjoying my first bath and it is pure and utter ecstasy.

'I'm returning!' I hear her giggle from the bedroom. 'Please ensure there are adequate bubbles present!'

I can't help but chuckle at her increased daring. Glancing down towards the soapy water I'm luxuriating in, I rearrange the bubbles strategically over the part of my anatomy I assume Clara's referring to...although I'm not entirely sure why she's being coy. It isn't as though she hasn't seen every part of me already, in her capacity as my nurse.

I know it sounds ridiculous, but it is blissful to be able to do something as simple as moving bubbles around the bath on my own. After a month of being permanently needy, the ability to use my limbs again feels like a real achievement. Of course, my legs aren't moving in anything like the way I need them to, but my arms are starting to come back to me properly again.

'I'm coming in,' Clara announces in a sing-song voice, managing to knock on the frame of the open bathroom door, while holding a hand over her eyes.

'Help yourself. I'm quite decent.'

She lowers her hand and we share a small smile, the candlelight flickering in her eyes. The various candles are not my idea but having hijacked the bathroom Clara's been using, it is naturally filled with the things she's brought with her, and that includes a hell of a lot of nightlights. I get the impression bubbles and candles are two of the great joys in Clara's life and to be honest they're quickly starting to become two of mine as well.

I guess I must be pretty relaxed because, thanks to regular hot water top-ups, I've already been in the bath for almost an hour. Initially, Clara sat beside me in my wheelchair, both of us reading.

With just the sound of our light breathing and the occasional page being turned, it really was quite an intimate atmosphere. But recently, she's been jumping up and down at intervals, attempting to cook dinner while keeping an eye on her troublesome patient who is showing no signs of exiting his dream bath. But then I've yearned for this experience for so long. I've endured long weeks of trying to ignore the pain and itchiness of my skin beneath plaster, which I just couldn't reach. I see this as my well-deserved reward and not something I'm willing to relinquish quickly.

'More hot water?' Clara suggests, proving that she understands me.

'You know what? I think I might get out soon.'

'Surely not!?' she teases gently. 'I expected you to be in here for at least another hour!'

'Maybe tomorrow,' I reply, pulling a face.

'Sounds like a plan,' she agrees. 'Now, do you think you can get yourself dry?'

You see, that's what I adore about this woman; she doesn't mollycoddle or pity me. Instead she bolsters me, continuously encouraging me to do things for myself. Yes, I've only just regained proper use of my arms but she's not allowing me to rest on my laurels. Heading back into her bedroom, she returns soon afterwards with a couple of towels and a change of clothes.

'Give me a shout if you need anything? I'm just in the kitchen.' And off she goes. Far from treating me like an invalid, Clara is allowing me to reclaim ownership of my own existence, along with my pride and self-worth. Attributes which, despite everyone's best intentions, had been stripped away from me before her arrival.

Having let the water out of the bath, I reach for one of the warm towels, pleasurably rubbing my face against the soft linen. It feels so good to have rinsed every last speck of my hospital visit away. I was only there for a few hours today, but still I'd felt the warm, antiseptic-smelling environment seeping back into my pores. It's certainly a relief to be clean again.

I discover my T-shirt is relatively easy to put on. It's a slower process to dry the rest of my body and get my shorts on, but the instant I do so, I feel a massive sense of achievement. Determined to take another leap forward in my recovery, I manage to exit the bath and shuffle myself into the electric wheelchair. Not that I intend to be dependent upon it for long, but it's a recent purchase to assist my movement around the house. Right now, my legs tire fast and have very limited strength. I know I need to build them up again... I know I need to be patient. It's just patience has never been a strength of mine, but I appreciate that it quickly needs to become one of my skills.

Beaming with pride, I manoeuvre the wheelchair into the kitchen minutes later to Clara's obvious astonishment and delight.

'Gosh! You really made me jump!' she exclaims, returning a baking tray to the oven.

'What's going on here?' I ask, astonished to discover my kitchen table decked out like a restaurant. It has a fancy tablecloth...goodness only knows where she found that...my best cutlery and crockery, a bottle of wine and the obligatory candle.

'It's a celebration dinner,' Clara explains.

'For what?'

'Well, it was going to be for the removal of your plasters but now, I actually think it needs to be for what you've just achieved in the last ten minutes. You're amazing!'

I feel my chest swell in response. I'm usually hopeless at accepting compliments but not this time. This time, I am rightly proud. Recently, I've been thrown through the wringer both emotionally and physically, but with Clara's help, at last I can see the light at the end of the tunnel. Pulling my wheelchair up to the table, I exhale deeply, feeling satisfied.

'Wine?' I offer, nodding towards the bottle which has already been left to breathe.

My pain medication is much reduced now, so alcohol is back on the menu in moderation. Who knows? One day soon I might even enjoy my wish of having a beer at the pub with a friend. And right now, I know exactly which friend I'd like that to be shared with;

Clara. For she is more than just my nurse, she is my friend, and I hope she always will be.

'That would be lovely, thank you,' she answers, bringing a beautifully presented first course to the table and sitting down beside me.

We enjoy a fantastic meal together that night; Clara certainly has many talents and I find myself wanting to discover everything I can about her. As a consequence, we barely draw breath, chatting continuously as we enjoy our celebration meal. Finally, the one subject I'd prefer wasn't on the menu was raised by Clara.

'I don't mean to be nosy but why doesn't your fiancée visit you anymore?'

'Please don't call her that,' I snap back, the thought of Henrietta instantly darkening my mood.

'I'm sorry,' says Clara quietly, bowing her head as though suitably chastised. But I don't want her to feel that way with me and given our growing closeness, it's only fair that she knows the truth.

'We aren't engaged,' I explain simply. 'Although obviously that's not public knowledge.'

'When did you break up?' she asks, looking astonished.

'A few hours after my accident, when she came to visit me in the hospital.'

'On whose request?' Clara's eyes are watchful now, her voice low and sombre.

'Hers.' Seeing the outrage in Clara's expression, I quickly jump in to clarify. 'But to be quite frank, when I saw the real person she was inside, I was immediately onboard with her suggestion.' I mean, of course I always knew Henrietta was somewhat superficial, but it was quite a shock to discover she was cruel and heartless too.

'You mean, she left you on the night of your accident, because you were injured? Because your new image didn't fit in with her perfect life?' Clara almost spat these words out in disgust.

'Yeah, that's about the size of it.'

I waver over whether to tell Clara the full story, before deciding not to. I don't wish to spoil our perfect evening by having to admit to the heart-wrenching truth. That thanks to my spinal damage, the doctor's warned me there was a fifty-fifty chance that my accident may have removed my ability to enjoy sexual pleasure. I guess I couldn't blame any woman for not hanging around in those circumstances...particularly a woman like Henrietta. Damaged and impotent; who the hell would want me as their lover?

NOT LONG AFTER our highly enjoyable dinner, we each turn in for bed. Having helped me into my own bed, Clara says goodnight and retires to her own room. Following a busy and somewhat emotional day, it is hardly surprising that I soon drift off to sleep. After what feels like only seconds later, I am being shaken by my shoulders, Clara's pleading voice filling my ears.

'Wake up, Brad! Wake up!'

'Whaa....?' I say stupidly, unwillingly opening my eyes against the dim light of the room. Suddenly, I realise my brow is beaded with sweat, my breath fast and gasping, as though I've run for miles. Images of being trapped in an enclosed box, with fingers of fire reaching towards my face, occasionally return into view.

'You were dreaming,' she explains, tenderly stroking the hair from my damp forehead. 'Here, have a drink.'

I manage to lever myself upright and sip from the glass she's offering.

'It was the accident,' I gasp, focusing my attention solely on Clara. I find looking at her is calming, providing a dependable, reliable presence amidst the swirling backdrop of my nightmares.

'Do you want to talk about it?' she asks, comfortingly stroking the back of my hand.

Instead of deferring to my reflex response that everybody else has received, I realise that the answer is yes.

'It was a private car race, between a small group of friends...that's the only reason it's been kept out of the papers for this long,' I explain, setting the background. 'I got cut up at one of the chicanes and the car went into a spin. I hit a nearby barrier at about a hundred miles an hour.' I swallow hard, remembering the scene clearly. 'When it finally came to a stop, I remember thinking I was lucky to still be alive and even more so, to be conscious, even though the car was crushed beyond recognition. And that's when I noticed the smoke.'

'Oh my God!' mutters Clara, her hand automatically clenching hard around my own. 'What happened?'

'Fortunately, one of my mates was really close by. He grabbed a fire extinguisher and managed to put it out, just as things were starting to get seriously frightening. To be honest, I thought I was a goner. I had to be cut out of the wreckage, from where I was taken to hospital. I guess it isn't surprising that it occasionally haunts my dreams.'

'Natural...perfectly natural,' explains Clara, her voice like a soothing balm to my soul. 'As with so many of these things, the psychological trauma can end up being much worse than the physical injury.'

'Is there anything I can get you?' she asks. Only then do I realise she's just wearing a pair of checked cotton pyjamas.

'There's one thing but...no...thank you.' I can't ask her for what I really need because I can't bear to risk our easy relationship.

'Tell me,' she demands. I recognise that tone. And I've heard enough of it over the past month to know that she expects a straight answer.

'I need a hug,' I admit.

Instantly, she throws an arm around my shoulder and pushes her head to my chest. Her proximity feels amazing, but this isn't what I had in mind.

'No,' I say gently. 'I mean, I need a *real* hug. I want to cuddle you in bed. Ideally all night.' There, I've said it. Now it's up to her to turn and run.

But to my delight and astonishment, Clara does neither of those things. Instead, she turns off the bedside light and crawls under the covers beside me.

'Thank you,' I whisper into her ear, as I pull her against my body, spooning from behind. For the longest time, I just hold her in my arms as she gradually falls to sleep. And I'm not afraid to admit that it feels incredible. As my weary mind finally shuts down, I become vaguely aware of a light tingling in my abdomen. A very distant ache. I must already be dreaming. And then the exhaustion of the day overwhelms me and I am consumed by sleep.

CHAPTER 5

CLARA

During the few days that follow my unexpected overnight stay with Brad, I do find myself rather going through the motions, in terms of how we interact. I know I'm putting a little distance between the two of us, and I wonder if Brad can feel it too. It isn't really being consciously done, but it was a shock to discover that he is no longer in a relationship with Henrietta. The truth is, I've been living with one understanding of our situation, and Brad's been living with quite another; he knew he was single and I knew he was engaged. Suddenly, I'm questioning every touch we've shared in the past month, every smile, every hug. I guess I just need a little time to reconcile everything and get my head around what's happened, because there's no doubt that we are already far closer than a nurse and her patient would traditionally expect to be.

My issue is that working with Brad in such intimate and close quarters is both a thrill and a complication. He's pretty much, hands down, the sexiest guy I've ever met. The more time I spend with him and get to know him, the more I like him...and I mean *really* like him. Of course, knowing that he was with Henrietta helped me to maintain a professional and emotional distance, but now he's admitted to not being engaged any longer, all previous barriers have unexpectedly been removed and I'm honestly not sure how to deal with that. So, in the short term, I'm just keeping my head down, continuing with my work, and trying to hide my feelings. The thing is, as a friend, I think he's starting to like me too. Certainly together we share lighthearted fun and great conversations, enjoying ourselves as much as Brad's recovery will allow. Some days are good for him, and some days are bad. It's something I accept, grateful that it's my job to help him through every day as best I can.

Fortunately, Brad's parents have been at the house a lot, which has helped minimise any awkwardness. I think they're happy about the way their precious son is being looked after and the progress he's making. Despite my confusion, I'm obviously continuing to do my absolute best to facilitate his recovery. And I think they can see that. I think Brad can see that too, so long as you ask him on a good day. Certainly, he's much improved since our first meeting. His skin is brighter, his eyes less tired and haunted, his movement improving every day, and that cheeky smile that's known across the world thanks to his racing career, is returning on a more regular basis than ever. Not that I ever knew the original version of Brad, but I do believe he's becoming more of the man he used to be. Unfortunately, every day he looks just as attractive as the man I'd previously seen on television. Not that I don't want him to recover, but being increasingly sexually attracted to Brad under these circumstances is not helpful.

'It's a lovely day,' I observe, one morning when Brad's parents aren't due to visit. 'And I do believe you still have a few wishes outstanding. Would you like to take a trip to the beach?'

'Not in the rustbucket?' he jokes, pulling a pained face at me, his fingers moving swiftly across the screen of his phone which beeps and buzzes at increasingly regular intervals these days. Obviously very popular, I don't doubt that Brad has a great number of friends. Part of me hopes that Henrietta isn't still one of the people he's regularly communicating with, but really, what business is it of mine? Hiding my thoughts, I laugh aloud, grateful that we are still able to have fun together and my recent behaviour hasn't ruined everything.

'Big Bertha is a very sensitive soul,' I reply. 'So unless you want her to break down while we're out today, simply to spite you, then I suggest you minimise your insults?'

'My wholehearted apologies to both you and Bertha,' says Brad, as we both grin cheesily at each other. 'Can you ever forgive me?'

'I'll consider it,' I admit. A look passes between us, which suggests our conversation might just have another meaning.

Within half an hour, I've packed up a picnic for the beach, helped Brad up the ramp into his least favourite vehicle, and we're on the road. It's another gorgeous summer's day and the air is already heating up. With the windows wound down, it's a joy to feel the warm air floating across my skin. I breathe out a huge sigh of satisfaction. Seconds later, I hear Brad's voice behind me.

'I'm sorry,' he says softly.

'I'm sorry too,' I admit, glancing at him through the interior mirror. For a second, our eyes lock, allowing our emotions to be laid bare.

'What do you have to be sorry for?'

I return my eyes to the road and grip the steering wheel a little more tightly. It feels as though I ought to be honest with him and besides, it's much easier to open your heart to somebody while you're driving than face to face, with no distractions.

'For being a bit distant. The news that you weren't with Henrietta anymore came as quite a shock and I've just been trying to get my head around stuff.'

'Why would you need to get your head around that news?' he asked, genuinely curious.

'Because I like you...' I croak, feeling a cold shiver traversing my spine.

'I like you too,' he admits, sending me a supportive smile.

'No, but I mean...I *really* like you.' Seeing Brad's face fall in disbelief, I swing my eyes back to the road, wishing I hadn't opened my big mouth. But having started, it felt sensible to at least complete my humiliation. Why the hell didn't we leave this conversation until the way back home? At least then, we wouldn't have to spend the entire day with each other feeling uncomfortable.

'Well, I'm the one who should be apologising,' Brad says at last, after what feels like a very long silence, but may well have only been a few seconds. 'I should have made my position clear earlier. There were times when I had the chance to do so, and chose not to. At first, it was because I didn't know if I could trust you. And then once I realised I could trust you, it just became more and more difficult to admit. I let it slide, and I shouldn't have. I'm really sorry.'

'It's not a problem,' I shrug. 'It doesn't matter.'

'It does to me. There's something else you ought to know too,' he sighs.

'Yeah?'

Then follows a pause so long that we practically reach the coast-line before one of us talks again. In desperation, I decide to fill the silence.

'Forgive me for being naïve or impertinent,' I begin.

'Or possibly both?' suggests Brad with a smile.

'Yeah, possibly,' I agree gratefully. 'But what's with all the secrecy? I can understand Henrietta not wishing to broadcast her actions to the world,' I admit. After all, she was the one who callously dumped Brad, just hours after his accident. 'But I don't understand why you feel the same way. I mean, it's been well over a month now and there hasn't been a sniff of anything in the media.'

'Well, it helps that the car racing season has come to a close, so I'm not required to make any appearances. This is traditionally the time of year that drivers fall off the grid for a while, so to speak. So my absence isn't surprising.'

'I just don't see the point in hiding it. There's no shame in what happened to you. People have accidents all the time. In fact, if you were to make public that you are suffering, you'd probably help a great deal more people than the next social media navel gazing exer-cise that Henrietta embarks on. She could even support you and show some real emotion for a change?'

'Real emotion?' baulks Brad, his laughter loud and genuine. 'I'm sorry. Are we talking about the same person here?'

'Don't be too harsh on her,' I chastise gently. 'After all, she did at least organise your care, by finding me.'

'True. That is the one thing I do have to be forever grateful about,' admitted Brad, his amusement fading. 'Although I'm convinced she only insisted on doing that, so that if our story ever does hit the papers, she can use it as her defence.'

'I'm sure she had her reasons,' I say, vaguely trying to remain neutral.

'She certainly did have her reasons,' Brad admits coldly. 'She couldn't deal with the man I'd become.'

I glance again at his face in my mirror, seeing only the attractive man that I have grown so very fond of. Yes, in the early days, the damage to his face had been pretty bad, but faces heal faster than just about any other part of the body, and I'd say Brad was at least eighty percent recovered already, with plenty of time ahead of him for further improvement. To me, he looks as handsome as ever...perhaps even more so, given the bad boy vibe the low level scarring suggests.

'Well, that was pretty short-sighted of her, wasn't it?' I shrug. Having made it to the beachfront, I'm thrilled to discover an ideally located parking space, which I start to reverse into. 'She must be kicking herself, given how handsome you look now!' I just about manage not to admit he looks fucking gorgeous; that would rather give my hand away completely.

'She only partly dumped me for my altered looks. Her main objection was the chance of me being impotent.'

A chill passes straight through me upon hearing these words and I'm instantly grateful that I've just turned off the ignition. Swallowing hard, I turn around in my seat to face Brad. He looks the very definition of dejected.

'I'm very sorry to hear that,' I say softly, touched that Brad has enough trust in me to admit it. 'But I didn't see that on any of your medical records.'

'No. You wouldn't have,' he confirms. 'I asked for it to be redacted.'

'Okay...and your reason?'

'Why do you think? Shame,' he admits with a long exhale. 'For the avoidance of humiliation in the press, if they ever got hold of the information.' Unfortunately, he has a point. Medical records are, of course, confidential, but no database is unhackable.

'What you have to understand about Henrietta,' Brad goes on to explain. 'She's all about the fast win, immediate gratification, be it physical, emotional or sexual. Everything in her life has to provide pleasure or she loses interest fast. I delivered what she needed very adequately until there was a risk that I couldn't. At which point, she wasn't willing to wait, help me, and see me through the uncertainty. Put simply, I became a complication that she wasn't able to accept.'

'Then you're much better off without her,' I state firmly, meaning it. Reaching towards him, I take hold of Brad's hand and squeeze it, attempting to ignore the rush of adrenaline which fills me, as our skin touches. 'I'm so sorry you were treated in such a cruel way. You don't deserve it.'

'Yeah, well, you might not have noticed but Henrietta Glover isn't known for her kindness. Oh no, but then of course she is! Her spotless media image means more to her than anything; certainly more than I ever did.'

I let Brad get everything off his chest, because I think he needs to. He might not be sitting on a cliff edge, screaming obscenities out to the ocean, but in its own way, this is equally as valuable.

'But most of all,' he concludes, determinedly rounding up our conversation. 'I'm sorry if I've upset you in any way. You see, you didn't need to worry about liking me, either a little or a lot. Even if I fully recover the use of my limbs, I'm unlikely to ever be able to satisfy a woman again, so please don't give me another thought.'

There is so much I want to say to Brad in response to that statement. So many ways I can argue that he's wrong. But I've seen that look of determination on his face before so regretfully I say nothing.

'Now, come on!' he says encouragingly, with what I recognise as false enthusiasm. 'I thought we were here to enjoy the beach? I don't put my shorts on for just anyone, you know?'

And to my enduring shame, I don't say anything to challenge his harsh and wholly incorrect assumption. Instead, I help him out of Bertha and we head towards the promenade.

CHAPTER 6

BRAD

Despite a rather rocky start, I've had an amazing day so far, enjoying a beer in a pub on the seafront, followed by fish and chips for lunch. Nobody could imply that Clara doesn't stand by her promises. One by one, she's delivered on each of the requests I made when we first met, and it means a great deal to me that she's trying so hard to improve my life and raise my spirits. A feat she achieves every single day, if only she realised. True, it isn't ideal being pushed helplessly along the promenade, when I'd rather be running about chasing her, and making her giggle as I pull her into my arms. But what we're enjoying is probably as much as I can expect these days. Just like I can't expect to be effortlessly attracting women any longer, in my weakened state.

At first, I did have a slight fear of being recognised, pulling my baseball cap lower over my nose than normal, but I've settled into the environment now. The beach is busy but most people are far too intent on enjoying themselves to worry about the fact that a sportsman they once saw on the television might be in the vicinity. Besides, I'm practically unrecognisable from the cocky person I once was, strutting around with Henrietta on my arm. The accident was undeniably a really shit thing to happen, but in a strange way, I think it's made me become a better person. I certainly appreciate life a damn sight more now, and see the value in having real, genuine people around me.

As we stroll, or in my case roll along the promenade, it's bliss to feel the warmth of the sun on the lower part of my legs and hear the sounds of waves splashing further down the long sandy beach. Part of me yearns to feel the sand between my toes again...maybe one day. Although the mobility of my legs noticeably improves every week, I am not yet able to walk any further than a few steps, although I can now stand unaided. But I certainly couldn't make it safely onto the beach, and the deep sand is hardly wheelchair-friendly.

'Can I abandon you here, just for a minute?' asks Clara, breaking my approaching melancholy.

'Sure,' I shrug as she sends me a warm smile and walks across the sand towards a group of young, fit and good-looking guys. And then I catch a glimpse into my future. Me stuck alone in this contraption, while she gets on with her life, meeting a decent man that I can never hope to measure up to. I know I mustn't be ungrateful, or complain too much, or depress everyone around me, and I do genuinely try to stay positive. I have so much to be grateful for. But just sometimes, at moments like this, I have to admit that things do get on top of me. Brushing away the liquid which is daring to pool at the base of my eyes, I set my features appropriately as I see Clara returning.

'Okay?' she asks, looking a little concerned.

'Of course,' I confirm with a small smile. 'Just soaking up the atmosphere. Did any of them ask you out?' I add teasingly, nodding towards the men she's just visited. For some reason, four of them are starting to rise to their feet.

'I'm not sure I'm quite their type,' she chuckles. 'At least ten years too old, for a start!' She bends down in front of my wheelchair and for some unfathomable reason, starts to take off my shoes and socks. Once upon a time, my legs would be shaking by now, but not today.

'What the hell are you doing?' I ask, with mock exasperation.

'Why are you so fucking argumentative?' laughs Clara.

'I've got to have control over some things, haven't I?'

'You've got control over a lot more than you think...'

'If you say so, Nursie!' I reply, playfully.

'Please don't call me that! Now, are you ready to go onto the beach?'

'No. Don't be silly. You can't possibly manage me,' I explain, shaking my head gently. 'Maybe another time in the future?' I say, trying to insert some hope into my tone.

'*I* might not be able to manage you, but *they* certainly can,' she smirks, nodding her head in the direction of the approaching men.

'You walked over to a group of strangers, to ask them to carry me onto the sand?' I ask in astonishment.

'I'll remind you that this is one of the wishes on your bucket list. And what kind of nurse would I be...what kind of friend would I be...if I didn't do everything I could to get this to happen?' she asks. 'Now, man up. They're coming over.'

'Man up?' I repeat in astonishment. That's something I've never been accused of not doing before. But she's correct. Not only must I face the fact that this is my new reality, but I also need to accept that life can be good if I just put some effort in. And I can't deny that life has certainly been good today.

Before I know what's happening, I've been introduced to a group of four really nice guys, who each take a corner of my wheelchair and lift both it and me into the air and across the sand. It's a slightly wobbly ride, and I won't deny I feel a damn sight safer back on solid ground, but it is certainly a thrill to be in the middle of a sandy beach, in the centre of everything.

'We're gonna be here all afternoon,' says the guy who previously introduced himself as Jez. 'So just give us a shout whenever you need a lift back again? We're very happy to help.'

Having thanked them, Clara and I settle down to enjoy some time on the sand. Managing to slip out of my wheelchair, I manoeuvre myself onto the beach towel she lays out for us to share. And there we sit for several hours, happy to sample the simple pleasures of life which I'd previously never given myself the time or opportunity to enjoy; building sandcastles, reading, chatting and pushing our feet into the deep, warm sand.

'This has been the best day in...I don't know how long,' I admit, as the sun starts its slow descent from high in the sky.

'Since your accident,' nods Clara.

'No.' I'm quick to correct her, keen to make her understand that today has meant more to me than she could possibly comprehend. 'No, before that. A *long* time before that. You make me feel free, Clara,' I try to explain, looking deep into her beautiful brown eyes. 'You make me feel like anything is possible.'

'Hey, come on, Bradley *Christian* Drake,' she smiles, giving my arm a playful push. Silently, I acknowledge that I'm not entertaining very holy, Christian or pure thoughts right now. 'Anything *is* possible where you're concerned; you're amazing!'

Almost outside of my control, my hand reaches out, capturing hers before she removes it.

'Thank you. This means more to me than you'll probably ever know.'

'You're welcome,' Clara replies shyly, as she recognises the sincerity in my tone. 'Is there anything else you need?'

'Yes,' I say decisively. 'I *really* need a hug.' And it's true; I really do.

Lying back on the warm towel I raise my arm, encouraging her to snuggle against my chest. When she does just that, it makes me feel as though I've won the lottery. I know I left it too long, but it is such a relief to have shared the truth with Clara. Everything is out in the open now; we have no secrets.

'Do you know, you've granted each and every one of my wishes over the past month?' I mutter against her hair, inhaling the sweet scent of her fruity shampoo, floral perfume and promise.

'I know! Just call me your fairy godmother,' she chuckles.

'If that's the case, I have a seventh and final wish,' I confess, the heat and longing within me at bursting point.

'Oh yeah?' she murmurs, sounding content.

'Yeah. Someone very special once told me that I have to fight for what I want in this world. Well, what I want is you.'

One day, I guess I'll learn to keep my thoughts to myself, but that probably isn't going to be any time soon. My admission immediately alters the tone of our conversation and I feel Clara's previously relaxed body starting to stiffen in my arms.

'I'm sorry. Please can we forget I ever said that?' I request with a sigh. 'Sometimes I just get caught up in the moment and forget who...and what I am now. Or rather, what I'm not.' I mean, what was I thinking? Clara wouldn't desire me, and if she did, I'd have to seriously question her sanity.

Turning around and breaking our close intimacy, she levers herself up onto one elbow and fixes me with a stern glare.

'Are you reverting to talking shit again, like you used to?' she queries. I've always greatly appreciated straight talking, but this is unusually straight, even for her. 'I feel surprisingly disappointed. I really had hoped you'd grown out of being that person...'

'Huh?' I reply, pulling myself into a sitting position, in order to face her head on.

'I know in your world, physical beauty can be everything, but that isn't true for everyone. Some of us find beauty in the souls that we touch, the people that we grow to like and love,' she explains passionately, making me feel increasingly guilty about my outburst. But she isn't done yet.

'Real life isn't all about who looks best on Instagram or in some beauty magazine. And the more you mature and see people age and fade around you, that's when real beauty can shine through. Think of Henrietta in fifty years' time...'

Instantly, a cool shiver passes through me. The last thing I want to think about on this happy day is my ex, whether that be the version of her today or in the future.

'I'd really rather not,' I admit.

'She won't have her looks then. I appreciate that plastic surgery is a booming business, but no matter what she does, she won't be able to reverse the ravages of time. But if the woman you loved had beauty bursting from inside her, would that matter to you?'

'No,' I reply with absolute certainty, not because I'm thinking about Henrietta in that moment, but because my mind is filled with Clara. 'No, it wouldn't matter at all.'

I guess Clara might have registered some unknown meaning in the tone of my response because she suddenly heads off on a minor tangent, as though to fill the distance between us with words.

'I don't understand why people are so obsessed about beauty. It's mostly all false anyway....filters and makeup and nips and tucks. That's all just bullshit!'

I really should have guessed that was Clara's stance before today. Of course, she has incredible physical beauty, but that's more thanks to the light she emits from within, and the way she carries herself, than any external features. Although, in my opinion, she is physically stunning too. But the clues that this is how she feels have always been there. You only have to take a look at that rustbucket van of hers. Although now I can see that even her vehicle is a reflection of her general principles and priorities in life.

I gaze at Clara, as though seeing her for the very first time with all her protective layers peeled away, but her focus has switched to the group of guys who helped me across the beach earlier.

'Excuse me,' she murmurs, rising to her feet. 'I think I should go and organise our lift before they leave.' And with that, I watch her walk away. I'm left wondering what answer Clara might have given to my seventh wish, if only I'd kept quiet a little longer and just allowed her to respond naturally.

LATER THAT SAME evening we're sitting in front of the television when there's a knock at the door.

'I'll go,' offers Clara, rising to her feet and walking out of the room. She returns a minute later carrying the most enormous bouquet of blooms and wearing a huge smile.

'Look at these beautiful flowers! Aren't they amazing?' she exclaims in delight, placing the box on the seat beside me. 'They came for you.'

'They're very pretty,' I agree. 'Please could you open the card?'

Clara fixes me with a stern glare, as though she's about to refuse. After all, I can perform tasks like that myself these days. Fortunately, she relents. I try to suppress a small smile, as she rips open the envelope and studies the card, her expression growing increasingly confused.

'I'm sorry I'm a knob,' she read.

'They're for you, Sweetheart,' I explain quietly. 'I'm sorry that I disappointed you. The truth is, I disappointed myself too and everything you said on the beach was entirely warranted.'

'How did you get these delivered?' she asks, obviously not willing to respond to my statement.

'I can send messages with my phone, now that I've got use of my hands again,' I smile, wiggling my fingers playfully in her direction. 'I can do all sorts.'

'I don't want to know!' she laughs, shaking her head in amusement and apparently reading sexual innuendo into a throwaway statement which wasn't meant in that way. For some reason, her error fills me with hope. 'Thank you. These are so beautiful,' she adds, more serious now.

'You're more than welcome.' The truth is, I'd have purchased her flowers every day, if I'd been able. 'Since your arrival, you have truly changed my life, Clara,' I admit, somberly. 'This is just the very smallest token of my appreciation.'

'I'm just doing my job,' she shrugs. Her statement isn't meant to wound me, but it does. Sometimes I get carried away and forget she's here because she's being paid.

'Yes,' I admit, feeling resigned. 'And you do it exceptionally well.'

'I'll...er...just go and put these in some water,' explains Clara, gathering up the blooms and heading out of the door, no doubt to escape the increasingly tense atmosphere. Silently, I vow that I'll learn to keep my thoughts to myself in the future.

CHAPTER 7

CLARA

Some weeks have passed since what I refer to as *the beach incident*. The truth is, Brad's confession took me by surprise. I'll admit it was a shock...a big shock. I had no idea that my own desires were reciprocated in any way. But as I lay there in his arms, his words slowly percolating my conscious mind, I dared to wonder about what could be. Unfortunately, seconds later the conversation took a completely different turn. And that's a turn which has never been rectified. Since then, we've just been carrying on as before, as though nothing was said that day. I know it's the coward's way out, but it does avoid any further ripples of discomfort between us. I guess if Brad ever re-states his feelings towards me, at least I'll be prepared. Although going by the way he's acting, I don't think that's likely, so instead we simply enjoy our incredibly close friendship that continues on unabated.

Pretty confident that I can hear Brad approaching the kitchen, I stifle a sigh and pour the prepared egg mixture into a heated frying pan. No longer in need of my bathroom, he's been enjoying his own shower once again. Every day, I see examples of how our bonds are slowly being decoupled and I fear the distance between us is growing. Of course, I should rejoice in his increased independence, and I honestly do, not least because it means I've done a good job. But equally, the change can be tough to take, especially when it will ultimately result in his absence from my life.

'Hey,' I say, glancing around to see Brad enter the room. Long gone is the wheelchair. Thanks to his determination, he's walking around on just one stick now; a little shaky, sure, but his overall improvement has been nothing short of phenomenal. Brad does still require occasional assistance, but in truth, that could be handled by regular visits from his parents. I can't imagine I'll be required for much longer. Indeed, I was surprised to be asked recently if I'd extend my contract for a further month.

'Hey you,' he replies, sending me a warm smile as he sits at the breakfast table.

'There's some post for you on the table,' I add, before returning my attention to the heating eggs, eager not to burn them.

Shortly afterwards, I place Brad's favourite breakfast of scrambled eggs on toast in front of him, and take an adjacent seat. Unusually, he doesn't immediately tuck in. Instead, his expression is focused and thoughtful upon a small card that he's holding.

'Is everything okay?' I ask, guessing that it probably isn't.

'I've received an invitation to a charity ball.'

'Wow. That sounds nice,' I reply enthusiastically. Although given I've never attended a ball, I'm probably not best placed to offer such positive declarations.

'It has the potential to be nice,' confirms Brad carefully. 'Although it comes with significant complications.'

'Well, you can always turn it down?' I suggest logically. 'What are the complications?'

'The event is a fundraiser for a local children's cancer ward,' he explains. 'I agreed to attend many months ago, but with the accident, I forgot about it. The charity is one that both Henrietta and I publicly supported when we were together. I have a duty to be there.'

'But it would be your first appearance in public since your accident, and a lot of questions would be asked?' I offer.

'Mmmm,' he confirms. 'It would also mean spending the evening in the same room as my ex.'

'That's a tough call,' I agree, not envying his decision.

'It's not really a call. It's my duty to do what I can to help those kids,' he shrugs. Instantly, I feel a warm glow radiating inside me. He is such a kind-hearted soul, and he proves that to me every day without fail.

Suddenly, as though his mind is made up, Brad places the invitation down on the table in front of me and enthusiastically begins to eat his breakfast. I glance down at it, between mouthfuls. An expensive, embossed affair, the invitation is for a ball taking place at a local stately home this very weekend.

'Of course, I'll need a partner,' acknowledges Brad. ' Would you do me the honour?'

'Me?!' I exclaim, almost choking on the orange juice I'm sipping. 'I'm just a nurse!'

'I think we both know you're a lot more than that,' he states, his tone unusually stern. 'And I have to admit, it's a little disappointing to hear you say that. You are not *just* anything. At a bare minimum, you're my good friend and invaluable companion during the last two very difficult months of my life. And in all honesty, I wouldn't have wanted to go through this with anyone else by my side.'

BY THE EVENING of the ball itself, I'm a quivering wreck of nerves. Not only have I never been to an occasion as formal as this, but I'm attending with Brad on my arm. It would be naïve to assume that questions won't be asked. After all, he is expected to attend the event with Henrietta and, given the animosity between the two of them, I can't imagine anyone's going to believe they're still together. And will it then follow that I am seen as the other woman, even though I've done nothing but care for him?

But despite my ridiculous level of apprehension, I do want to accompany Brad, both for him and for myself. We deserve to share the remarkable achievement that he's made to get this far. Sure, Brad might not be dancing a great deal tonight, but he's going to be moving around on just a single walking stick. From the position he was in when we first met, to the place he's in now, that really is a remarkable achievement and testament to his determination to recover.

I glance in the mirror one final time, scarcely recognising the wide-eyed woman staring back at me. Surprisingly satisfied with my appearance, I'm wearing light makeup, my hair piled attractively on my head. But without doubt, the piece de resistance is my shimmering, gold dress. It was delivered to the house two days ago and is made of the most luxurious, undoubtedly expensive fabric I've ever touched, never mind worn. Brad instantly denied all knowledge of the garment but, of course, I know he purchased it. Fitting like a glove, as I move around it feels almost like a second skin. And I feel beautiful in it. No, more than that; I feel sexy. The transformation is incredible.

Purposefully inhaling a deep breath, I nervously make my way towards the kitchen where I can hear Brad moving around. As I step into the room, our eyes instantly lock and for a short while there is complete silence. I guess I should be getting used to the experience by now, but he dazzles me. Bradley Drake is, hands down, the sexiest guy I've ever seen in my life. Apparently born to wear black tie, with his hair tousled to perfection, he is the epitome of the handsome man I've previously seen on the covers of various magazines. For a brief and strange moment, it feels as though he is a stranger standing before me. As though I don't know this version of him at all. Even though the truth is, right now, I probably know him better than any person alive.

'You look....' Brad doesn't get any further than that. Walking unsteadily towards me, he takes me easily into his arms and holds me close as I melt like an ice cube on a hot day. 'Clara. You are absolutely stunning,' he groans beside my ear, his warm breath falling across my shoulder like a lover's caress.

Instantly I feel my heart descend into free-fall, my breaths becoming fast and shallow. I want to remain here forever, pressed close, luxuriating in his powerful, masculine presence. But it isn't long before he takes a step back, leaving me mourning the closeness of our bodies.

'Thank you for doing this for me tonight.'

'You're welcome,' I just about manage to mutter. 'And you look perfect.' I send him a small smile, but inside my heart is breaking. Henrietta is a famous and incredibly beautiful woman who, so I'm given to understand, tends to get what she wants. And with Brad almost one hundred percent recovered now, will she see him tonight and fall in love with him all over again? I couldn't blame her if she did. There will be plenty of women queueing up for a slow dance with this man tonight. I have no doubt.

———

BRAD HAS HIRED a driver to take us. I'm not sure if that's a blessing or a curse but, either way, we end up travelling the majority of the short journey largely in silence. Occasionally glancing at each other, our bodies close but not touching, I am hyper-aware of his presence.

'Everything okay?' he asks gently, just as we pull between two enormous wrought-iron gates and into what I can only describe as parkland.

'Sure,' I say, attempting to put a brave face on it, before almost immediately changing my mind and deciding to be truthful. 'I just hope I'm not out of my depth socially.'

'You most certainly won't be,' Brad assures me supportively. 'And besides, I don't intend to leave your side all night.' His admission causes me to inhale swiftly. I could read a number of implications into that statement, but I decide to translate it into the platonic, supportive version.

Our car pulls up in front of an enormous stately home and we carefully make our way into the main ballroom. There must be in excess of two hundred people present, all dressed in their finery and dripping with expensive jewellery. Diamonds seem to encrust every wrist and neck line and I don't doubt the wealth and importance of many of the guests. But Brad is welcomed like a long-lost friend. Within seconds of arriving, we each have a glass of champagne in our hands and Brad is bombarded with questions about his health and the reason he is using a walking stick. Proving himself to be both as popular and charming as ever, he provides suitably vague answers and is soon surrounded by an adoring crowd. Not touching, I remain by his side, not attempting to draw attention to myself.

Unexpectedly I feel a cold shiver pass through me, as I realise that Henrietta has just arrived, late but very much present, on the other side of the room. Not dissimilar to a heat-seeking missile, she wastes no time in identifying our location, making her way to Brad's opposite side. To my enormous surprise, they kiss each other on the cheek.

'Darling,' she purrs. 'You look incredible.'

'Thank you. And you look nice too, Henrietta,' he replies.

I'm not sure I've ever heard such a major understatement in my entire life; the woman looks stunning. She's like a tropical bird of paradise in an aviary shared only with monotone sparrows, standing out above every other woman. And that certainly includes myself. She is exquisite and I try my best not to hate her.

'Mmmm,' she groans seductively, squeezing his arm. 'And you've been working out.' A streak of something which feels suspiciously like jealousy flashes through me. Under my instruction, Brad has worked hard to maintain his muscle mass. He didn't let himself go, as it would have been so easy to do in his situation, but instead did everything I asked to fight, ensuring that the strength of his upper body in particular was well-maintained. Of course, his success in that area was helped by the fact that he's probably the most determined man I've ever met before in my life. But I'll admit, I hadn't expected one side-effect of his hard work would be to enable Henrietta *bloody* Glover to publicly fawn all over him.

But the thing that's causing me the most pain is a slow drip of realisation that Brad isn't pushing her away, and I don't understand why. I know he thinks Henrietta is poisonous...or at least, I thought he did. Perhaps he's trying to maintain their public image for the sake of the charity? Or is it something more macabre? After all, what man could honestly reject such beauty? And then suddenly, Henrietta releases Brad and focuses her considerable charms upon me, leaving me wondering if I haven't perhaps misjudged her.

'I can't thank you enough for taking such incredible care of Brad,' she murmurs. Her voice is so quiet that I doubt anybody else can hear us, but she does sound genuinely grateful. 'I expect he'll be recovered enough for me to look after him soon, but if you ever need a reference for future work, I'm more than happy to provide one.'

'Thank you,' I stutter. Nothing could have put me more firmly in my place than those few well-chosen words. However, she's not done turning the knife just yet.

'Now Clara, I must introduce you to Jackie Swift,' Henrietta announces, her voice miraculously returning to its standard volume. Henrietta sends a smile towards a plain woman standing just behind us, who looks almost as much out of her depth as I feel. 'Jackie is the Head of the Charity Board. And Jackie, this is Clara; the most incredible nurse we've been lucky enough to employ, during Brad's recovery.'

I'm feeling seriously confused. Henrietta is giving every indication that she and Brad are still together, and the situation is causing both my heart and my brain to ache. But it matters not. Soon after introductions have been made, Henrietta backs away from us, no doubt so she can go back to appropriating all of Brad's time.

Fortunately, it isn't long before dinner is served, and I find myself seated next to Brad and a long way away from Henrietta. Despite being as attentive as possible, he continues to be pulled in all directions and I feel the eyes of some predatory females upon me, no doubt wishing they inhabited my seat instead. I certainly underestimated the guy's popularity. To me, he's always just been plain old Brad; my friend and companion over the past few months. But these people act as though he's a superstar. I admit I'd forgotten that part of his personality during our time together...and I'd forgotten it to my detriment. Tonight he is very much public property, unsurprisingly drawing looks of both admiration and desire from a significant number of guests. Although it has to be said that a hefty proportion of that desire stems from Henrietta herself.

After enjoying an exquisite meal, waiters materialise from out of nowhere to clear down the tables, pushing the furniture to the outer edges of the room in order to make way for the main event; the dancing. While they're working, my new acquaintance Jackie Swift commandeers the microphone to much applause, focusing her thanks towards who she refers to as "our golden couple". Hearing her speak of Henrietta and Brad's *close bond* makes me feel somewhat nauseous and I find myself staring hard at one of the flower displays, determined not to look towards Brad.

'And we've learnt tonight that our dear patron, Bradley Drake, has recently suffered an accident,' Jackie goes on to conclude. 'But I'm sure that thanks to Henrietta's loving support, he's well on the mend now. So, if it isn't too much to ask, might the two of you be willing to open the dancing for us tonight?'

Immediately, the heat rushes from my body. Devoid of emotion, I watch Brad nod graciously and stand, before walking towards Henrietta with a single walking stick. An adoring smile spreads across her flawless features as she approaches him stealthily, like a predatory tiger, eyeing up the prey she is undoubtedly still attracted to. Meeting on the edge of the dance floor, an expressionless Brad offers out an arm and relinquishes his walking stick, and together they take centre stage once again. The crowd explodes in rapturous applause as the apparently devoted fiancée assists her handsome partner slowly around the room, swaying in time to the slow, romantic song being played by the live band. It's certainly an endearing image, but one I wish I'd never had to witness.

I secretly hope the torture will stop at the end of the first dance. Only then do I see Henrietta intimately whisper something into Brad's ear, and instead they continue dancing. My heart breaks. I simply can't bear to watch any longer. Making my excuses, I hold my head high and walk out of the room, aiming for the ladies. But en route, I change my mind, realising that I don't want to be here any longer. And I'm certainly not required. Grabbing my coat from the cloakroom, I head outside into the cool night air, striding towards our car. All the way home, I keep a lid on my emotions; a mask to hide my pain. Only when I'm safely back in my own bedroom do I finally break down. He is lost to me forever.

CHAPTER 8

BRAD

Silently gritting my teeth, I exhale slowly, reminding myself that I need to do my bit, which includes putting on a brave face for the sake of the charity. And that's what I've done. In a few minutes, Henrietta and I can go our separate ways and nobody will be any the wiser. So I continue to rotate around the dance floor, Henrietta's potent, musky perfume filling my mind with a myriad of bad memories, while I struggle to ignore her insistent caress of my lower back.

'Allow your hand to drop any further and I walk,' I mutter against her hair, meaning every word. She's starting to push me too far now. When we were together, Henrietta never attempted to hide the admiration she had for my ass, or stop prattling on about how she enjoyed the best sex of her life with me, but she can keep her damn hands to herself now. Although the truth is, and I know it's probably petty, but I'm pleased to remind her of what she's missing; to show her what she's lost and can never have again.

Over the top of Henrietta's head, I glance towards our table, only to note that Clara is missing. I assume she's gone to the ladies and try not to let her absence interfere with my equilibrium. But the truth of the matter is, I could really do with her calming presence right now. I also have a desire for Clara and I to share our first dance together, although silently I acknowledge that doing so publicly might not be the best idea I've ever had. You see, over the past few weeks, the most amazing thing has happened which is both a blessing and a curse. My physical sexuality which I'd feared had forever left me, has awoken once more and I'm regularly growing almost unbearably hard.

It isn't a reaction I'm likely to experience while dancing with Henrietta, of course, but it's quite a different matter when I'm at home near Clara. Obviously, this represents a major leap forward in my recovery which I would ideally wish to share with my carer, but I haven't dared to mention it. Medically, I'm sure Clara would be interested, but on a purely emotional level, I would hate her to think there was another purpose behind me sharing this information. To say life is super-complicated is a gross understatement. I'm only grateful that Clara no longer needs to nurse me so intensely, so I don't believe she's aware of this significant change which is making my life hard...in every sense of the word.

To my intense relief, the song comes to an end and I step away from Henrietta, adamant that she won't persuade me to remain for yet another dance. I guess she reads the determination from my demeanour, so chooses another tack instead. And damn her, she's right.

'You should dance with Jackie Swift.'

With a sharp nod, I turn away and do just that. Grateful to be out of Henrietta's unwelcome clutches, I request the pleasure of Jackie's company for the third dance. Not that what I'm doing can really be described as dancing, but at least I'm making the effort. As we circle slowly around the floor, I glance furtively towards our table again, starting to become concerned that Clara still hasn't returned. I hope she's okay. It's almost entirely down to Clara that I've come this far at all and I would love to celebrate my success with her. So, as soon as the song comes to an end, I ask a favour of the obliging Jackie.

'I'm really starting to worry where Clara is,' I admit, trying to keep my tone light. 'Is there any chance you could just go and see if she's in the Ladies, please? She's been missing for a little while.'

'Of course, leave it to me,' replies Jackie, sending me a supportive smile. But when she returns, her smile has gone. Instead, she simply shakes her head gently. 'I'm sorry, but I'm afraid Clara wasn't there.'

Bollocks. Has she gone because I've fucked up? Perhaps I should have refused to dance with Henrietta, or at least explained the position to her. I hope to God she doesn't think there's anything going on between us. I thought Clara understood; that most of my relationship with Henrietta was simply an act, and tonight was just another extension of that. Grabbing my phone, I call Clara, but receive no response. So instead, I tie things up as quickly as I can, make my excuses that I'm tiring, given that this is my first outing since the accident.

Having ascertained from my driver that Clara has indeed left, I take a lift home. Shuffling into my house minutes later, I discover the woman I adore sitting in her fluffy bathrobe and a nightshirt. With her makeup removed and long hair hanging loose around her shoulders, she is curled up on the sofa watching television. Clara looks infinitely beautiful, and my heart automatically starts to ache, along with other more demanding parts of my body. Glancing up, she looks shocked by my appearance.

'I'm so sorry! I didn't realise you were going to be home this early.'

Something tells me that she'd have made herself scarce if she had known.

'Why did you leave?' I demand. 'Why the fuck did you go without even saying goodbye?'

'You were...otherwise engaged,' explains Clara, obviously selecting her words with care. 'I didn't think you needed me.'

'You didn't think I *needed* you?' I repeat, unsure whether any words could be further from the truth. What the hell? Grabbing the remote control, I exchange the background television noise for a slow song on the radio. 'I'll tell you what I do need. What I've needed all night. And that's to dance with you.'

'What? Now?' She glances down at her attire in questioning disbelief, but I am not to be swayed.

'Right now,' I confirm. Holding out my hand, I feel a burning desire take hold of my chest as Clara accepts it. Her skin feels so soft, sliding against my own, it almost makes me want to weep with longing. Pulling her against my hardening physique, we sway together, as I lightly nuzzle the top of her head.

'You didn't think I needed you?' I murmur adjacent to her ear. 'I need you beyond anything. You're the reason I'm here. The reason I've got through this and have the drive to carry on.'

'But...' she attempts to interrupt, but I'm having none of it.

'There are no buts,' I say firmly, as she raises her gaze to lock with mine. 'I want you. I want to be with you. The big question is, do you want me too? Or am I just deluding myself?'

'I want you too,' confirms Clara. And then, as naturally as breathing, our mouths fall together.

It's a kiss I've dreamed of for months now, throughout the entire time we've been tiptoeing around each other, carefully keeping our distance. But not any longer. Kissing this woman is an utterly blissful activity, and one that I intend to be doing as often as possible from now on. The steady pressure in my groin has grown into a powerful, all-encompassing throbbing which fills me with a carnal hunger. I have an urge to bury myself deep inside Clara. It's a powerful desire which I can scarcely put into words. I allow the sensations to carry me away but when my tongue eventually probes gently against hers, our bodies reposition slightly and Clara receives first-hand evidence of the most recent advance in my recovery.

In astonishment, she breaks our kiss and glances down between us, to discover my black trousers are excessively tented. With a look of incredulous delight etched upon her face, she returns her eyes to mine.

'Well, that's unexpected,' she announces, the amusement evident in her tone.

It isn't exactly unexpected as far as I'm concerned, but still. Immediately, we start to laugh, breaking the tension that had been building between us. Pulling her back against me, I hold on tight to the most precious thing in the world. The woman I want to be with.

'That must be such a relief,' she admits. 'I'm so happy for you.'

'I'm happy for me too,' I grin. 'But be happy for both of us. After all, you're going to benefit equally as much as I will.'

'I am?' she asks coyly.

'Yeah, definitely. If you'll come to bed with me?' I murmur. God only knows how long I can maintain this erection for, but I intend to make the most of it while it's here. One thing my accident has taught me to do is live in the moment. Perhaps my attitude has rubbed off onto Clara, but even I'm surprised by the certainty of her response.

'Yes please.'

With our fingers entwining seductively, we walk slowly towards my bedroom, the promise of intense pleasure guiding our way. But just as we cross the threshold, there's an almighty rapping on the door.

'Get yourself into bed,' I request, dropping a kiss on the crown of Clara's head. 'I'll deal with this.'

'Do you have to?' she moans, obviously as keen as I am for our explorations to restart again as soon as possible.

'I'll be two minutes max. I promise.' I'm confident I won't be any longer, because I'm pretty sure I can identify the source of the disturbance. Sure enough, I pull open the front door to discover none other than Henrietta standing on the doorstep. Swathed in expensive fabrics, she has obviously just travelled directly from the ball.

'Darling!' she exclaims, attempting to look concerned but not entirely succeeding. 'Where did you get to? I was so worried!'

'I came home,' I say, somewhat redundantly given where we're standing. 'And I'm just about to go to bed, so if you don't mind...'

'May I come in?' Henrietta requests. 'Please,' she adds, when it becomes obvious that I'd rather she didn't.

'For what possible reason?' I enquire, trying to keep the anger from my voice. I see her hungry, eager little eyes slide down to my groin for a second, before returning to my face, this time accompanied by a small smirk. She mistakenly thinks my bodily responses are due to her arrival, but she couldn't be more wrong. This was one hundred percent caused by the dance Clara and I recently shared. My body and brain are continuing to buzz so much that my cock hasn't settled down again yet, although I have to say that Henrietta's unexpected appearance is certainly helping to speedily reverse that situation.

'I thought the doctors said...' she begins, before her words dry up.

'Yeah, well the doctors said a lot of things, didn't they?'

'I want you back,' admits Henrietta, casually forgetting everything that has previously passed between us.

'What? Because I'm physically capable of fucking you again? You do know love doesn't work that way, don't you?'

At long last, I can see straight through the woman. Shallow, narcissistic and surprisingly cruel, Henrietta is the polar opposite of Clara. What a blessing it is to have a woman in my life now who is honest, good and truthful. I have absolutely no desire for things to go back to the way they were with Henrietta, although she obviously doesn't share my view.

'I know you want me.' The arrogant tone of her challenge implies that she's the authority on my emotions. 'You can't escape the inevitable.'

I square my shoulders to face her directly. Something tells me that I'm going to enjoy making my position crystal clear.

CHAPTER 9

CLARA

Gently shaking all over, my heart is fluttering crazy fast. At Brad's insistence I'm in his bedroom, but I certainly haven't got as far as his bed. On the contrary, I'm hovering by the closed door, trying my very best to listen in on his conversation as the confidence I'd been experiencing quickly drains away. Although the words being shared between Brad and our late-night visitor are muffled, it doesn't take a great deal of imagination to guess who it is, or why she's here. Henrietta has appeared in order to reclaim her lover...the man who has just turned my body to warm liquid and set my senses on fire from a single kiss. And what a kiss! I'm honestly not sure I'll ever be the same again.

Just then I hear approaching footsteps and hurry away from the door, lest I'm caught eavesdropping. By the time Brad enters the room, I'm loitering ineffectually between the door and the bed, making it pretty obvious what I've been doing. I'm not sure whether he means to do so, but closing the door behind himself provides a silent statement of intent which only multiplies my shuddering; Brad still wants me to remain in his bedroom with him. He sends me a gentle smile but, possibly perceiving my uncertainty which I don't doubt is etched into my features, he doesn't approach further.

'Was that...?' I start, sounding awestruck.

'Yeah, it was,' he confirms, knowing exactly who I'm referring to.

'What did she want?'

'The one thing she can never have...me.'

'Oh...' I mutter, my gaze naturally falling to the ground. It's just too much to keep looking at Brad. Too damn intense.

'Because if you'll have me, Clara, I'm yours.'

'You can't mean...' I start to mutter, tears daring to well in my eyes. 'I'm a nobody in comparison to her. I'm just a nurse.'

Instantly, Brad is across the room, guiding me to sit on the edge of the bed as he takes me into his arms.

'But I do want you, Sweetheart. You're all I can think of,' he admits in gentle, honest tones. 'You fill my every waking moment. And at the end of the day,' Brad adds, putting on a surprisingly good American accent which has the unexpected effect of turning me on further. 'I'm just a boy, sitting in front of a girl, asking her...'

'Oh stop!' I start to laugh, in spite of myself. 'You're no Julia Roberts!'

'I'm not sure how to take that statement!' he grins, lifting my hand in order to place a gentle kiss against my palm. His warm, slightly moist lips send an instant shiver of longing straight through me and, despite my reservations, a light moan escapes from my throat.

'Say you'll stay with me tonight.'

'I suppose I could, if you insist,' I gasp, as Brad's talented mouth makes its way to the delicate skin on the inside of my wrist, making me squirm slightly. He is weaving his spell once again, and I am powerless to resist.

'Don't be too keen,' he smirks, gently encouraging me up the bed. 'You might give me a complex.'

'I think you've probably got quite enough self-belief.'

'Don't be so sure,' he growls. And then, almost as though we are destined to be united, our trembling lips combine once more.

Our kiss is soft and gentle but loaded with promise, as we spend plenty of time simply becoming acquainted with each other. While he runs a caressing hand over my back and occasionally my ass, my fingers tentatively explore his head, chest and arms. It's strange because I know his body so well as a nurse, but as a lover I am touching Brad for the very first time. And it feels amazing. Intense, but amazing. And with every passing minute, I can feel him growing harder, his thick cock wedged against my thigh, with various layers of clothing continuing to separate us.

Breaking our connection, Brad drops a line of kisses across my face to my ear, before seductively sharing his observations.

'You're shaking, Baby.' His tone is low and gravelly, oozing further evidence of how incredibly turned on he is. 'Would you like me to drive you to the coast, so that you can scream towards the heavens and release some tension? Or will you permit me to cause an entirely different kind of screaming right here in my bed?'

'Brad!' I mutter, shocked at his directness. But my reaction is subsumed by a great, shuddering gasp, as his fingers creep under the hem of my nightshirt for the first time, heading for a location which is already throbbing for relief.

'Oh God!' I groan, his fingers playfully investigating my sensitive thighs, before daring to stroke rhythmically across my mound. If he thought I was shaking a minute ago, that is absolutely nothing compared to the state he's got me into now. I can feel the muscles in my neck straining as my spine twists and curves in response to his incredibly tender touch. Through the low lighting, I glance into his eyes and am overwhelmed by a loving intimacy that all but takes my breath away.

'Shhh,' he soothes, his fingers never pausing in their wickedly effective actions. The pressure is already verging on being over-whelming, making me yearn for so much more. 'You can relax. I'm not going to be rushing you, or indeed us. I don't intend to make love to you until I understand what turns you on the most...until I know *exactly* what you need from me.'

Fuck.

And Brad soon proves that he means every word. Spending a frus-tratingly long time simply stroking every inch of my skin, except where I most need him to provide relief, it isn't long before I'm squirming and groaning beneath his fingers and mouth, urgently begging him for more. With my nightclothes long since discarded, my aching breasts are fully exposed to him, my legs wide open, and still he refrains from touching, instead leaving me highly frustrated and literally dripping with arousal.

'Please,' I moan. It isn't the first time I've made such an impassioned plea, but this is certainly the most desperate-sounding.

'Give me your hand,' Brad requests throatily.

Quivering beyond belief, I do as he asks, touched by the tender way his hand encompasses the back of mine. Then, without fully appreciating what he's doing before it's too late, he pushes down the rest of my digits so that only my index finger remains, before dipping it gently between the drenched, swollen folds of my pussy. Instantly, I cry out in both appreciation and surprise, as the intensity all but overwhelms me. But he's not done yet. Taking charge of my wet finger, he smears the arousal around one of my achingly hard nipples, making me cry out with an urgency of need I don't ever remember experiencing before. And then, accompanied by the cheekiest smile, his lips encompass my throbbing nipple and I disintegrate beneath him.

The feelings are like nothing else on earth, as his talented mouth caresses, building up my pleasure with rhythmical strokes. But what really catapults my self-control out onto the very edge is the sound of Brad's low, pleasurable groans, as his tongue consumes greedily, and he tastes my arousal for the very first time.

'Mmmmm, more,' he utters, his eyes looking almost intoxicated with lust. 'Feel how turned on you are.' Taking my finger again, this time he drags it all the way through, to finally slide across my engorged clit. Aware of the arousal already flowing onto the sheets below, I feel astonishingly wet; almost obscenely so. The impact causes my entire being to tremble in response, forcing me to release a cry which is sharp and pitchy.

'What have you done to me?' I gasp. The truth is, I've never felt my pussy so swollen before, almost as though there is too much blood attempting to pump through it. If that's the case, it certainly explains why my head is so goddamn fuzzy.

'I haven't done anything...yet,' Brad mutters as this time, he rubs my finger around my other nipple, before lowering his head to feast. 'I'm just learning to read your body.'

If that's seriously the case, I think, as his warm lips pull my needy flesh into his mouth, then he's already dangerously fluent. Suddenly, I make a noise like a wild animal. Convinced I feel the graze of his teeth against me this time, I can't contain my response to the corresponding sensations which flutter across my clit. Kissing a path towards my mouth, he releases my finger, to enable his own hand to take over.

'Oh fuck!' I mutter. I'm not sure I can cope with the pleasure over-load which is currently ravaging through me, but as my legs naturally stretch open wider to enable Brad to touch me fully, I discover I'm beyond caring.

Softly, his mouth claims mine at the same time as I feel his fingers stroking through my plentiful arousal. I recognise the faint taste of myself on his tongue, as it sweeps through my mouth, heightening the already overwhelming bliss being provided by his fingers. Moaning almost continuously by this stage, I sense Brad's fingers playfully moving like silk through my swollen folds, proving himself capable of making me shudder at the smallest of touches. Occasionally, his soft kiss briefly deepens, while his long fingers dare to probe.

Feeling as though we are living in a slow-motion world, I'm strug-gling to comprehend just how tender Brad is being. He's also showing an unbelievable level of restraint. Going without sex for chunks of time isn't exactly unusual for me, but I get the impression that the months Brad has recently gone without sexual intimacy, is out of the ordinary for him. Just from the continued presence of his heavy erec-tion and the throaty groans he occasionally emits, I sense he is abso-lutely brimming over with sexual desire, no doubt desperate for release. But still he seems determined to progress at a gentle pace, never once rushing us through the various stages of our joint plea-sure. Brad is visibly savouring the effect he has on me. The way he is capable of making me spasm with the most inconsequential of touches, before enjoying each and every one of the breathy moans that spontaneously follows.

As I shake out of control, Brad draws back slightly to enable our eyes to lock once more. Watching each other closely, I feel the growing intensity of our connection, as his hand moves to reposition his thumb directly over my clit. A gasp escapes my open mouth, as he presses down gently but firmly with gradually increasing insistence, before just holding still. Instantly, I feel the tension within my abdomen start to grow; a sensation which is magnified considerably, when Brad starts to move his thumb in the minutest circles.

'Oh!' I whimper, unable to cope with what he's doing. Incredibly, I can feel a building pressure that I can't contain for long, as my pussy starts to stream for him. A trembling takes over as my hips naturally grind, further increasing the thrill and making my fast-approaching release nothing but an inevitability.

'Look at me,' he orders, the instant my eyelids threaten to flicker shut. He sounds just like the Devil himself. 'Watch me closely.'

'Oh God!' I grunt, my body starting to convulse, as he apparently alters exactly how he will torment me, based solely upon my responses. I can't bear it. I can't do as he asks. I just can't cope. Seconds before my eyes roll closed and ecstasy takes hold, I see Brad's mouth open, taking one of my nipples confidently inside. And then he applies a divine compression which moves me to a different plane entirely. With a roar so loud that I even surprise myself, my extended orgasm is violent, noisy and incredibly intense, enabling me to explode with sheer elation. Brad's fingers never pause. Peaking endlessly, held utterly within his control, it is the longest time before I am eventually allowed to descend from that mammoth high.

'That's my good girl,' Brad praises softly, nudging his face against my glowing, reddened cheek. 'Although, given how enjoyable that sounded, I think you should have another, don't you?'

CHAPTER 10

BRAD

Clara's cries of passion and intense satisfaction are like nourishment to my spirit and only encourage me to continue, ravenous as I am in my desire for her. Initially, I might have been concerned about how long my erection would last, but not any longer. I've been rock hard for well over half an hour already, with no suggestion that position will change. Indeed, the longer I spend in this incredible woman's company, the more determinedly I want to fuck her. Although of course, *fucking* isn't the correct terminology to use where we're concerned. What we're sharing feels more like a meeting of two souls. We were already such close friends before today, that any physical coupling was only ever going to result in a glorious union of two people that completely adore each other.

Kissing across the incredibly soft skin on her abdomen, I descend lower, to hover over her swollen, wet pussy, asking a question I already know the answer to.

'Are you sure you want this?'

'For fuck's sake, *please*,' Clara moans urgently, her fingers winding through my hair in an attempt to trap me into position. It's a temptation I'm never going to be able to resist. So with a groan of deepest euphoria, I encourage my tongue to gently flicker and glide against her. Unable to prevent herself, she cries out with desire; she's been visibly turned on since we tumbled into bed, but she is positively pounding with an urgency to be fucked now. There is no denying the needs of this extraordinary woman. She can attempt to hide it all she likes, but I can see exactly what she requires and I plan to do my best to provide it.

Eager for much, much more, I dip my tongue deeper this time, her body correspondingly tensing in reaction, as another cry fills the otherwise silent air. Her arousal tasted ridiculously good earlier when I sucked it from her nipples, but enjoyed directly from the source, her juices are like honey sliding across my taste buds. My drug of choice, I instinctively know that I'll never get enough of Clara. And as much as I want to bury myself inside her, I also just want to hold her. To love her.

This woman was designed to enjoy pleasure, and it's the biggest thrill to slowly discover each of Clara's desires. The way her hands clench when I suckle her clit, her tell-tale low moans as my fingers curl deep and encourage her to come apart for me over and over again. For as much as I adore chatting to Clara, and I honestly do, I'm quickly discovering that I enjoy pushing her boundaries even more. There is no greater thrill than rendering her incoherent with joy.

Having reduced Clara yet again to a shuddering, squirming version of her former self, I retract. Kissing my way back up her delectably soft skin, I only pause when I am once more gazing deeply into her eyes.

'Tell me you're okay?' I request. I have to be sure this is still what she wants.

'I'm a lot more than okay,' she giggles, a massive grin exploding across her face. 'I'm absolutely fucking fantastic!' Instantly my expression changes to match hers.

'I'm very pleased to hear that, Sweetheart.'

'There's just one problem,' she admits, instantly causing me concern.

'And what's that?'

'I feel like I'm missing out on some of the fun,' she says, her eyes sparkling with glee. I'm not sure exactly what she's referring to, but I know there are some incredibly naughty thoughts currently scuttling through her mind. I quickly discover what she means as Clara rises up onto her knees to turn her attention to my clothing. The look on her face is priceless and I feel like a much sought-after Christmas present being unwrapped.

Having discarded my shirt, Clara places soft kisses all over my torso, slowly working her way downwards until she reaches the waistband of my trousers. With a smirk, she dips lower still, grazing her teeth along the substantial bulge in my trousers.

'Oh my God,' I mutter in shock, as her face remains on that level and she starts to unfasten my remaining clothing. Does she intend to do what I think she does? Henrietta was all about receiving pleasure, but giving it was never her forte. As a result, I can't actually remember the last time I was with a woman who wanted to reciprocate in this way. By the time Clara starts to peel the remaining clothing from my body, I am physically trembling. I can't think straight. I can't even think crooked. Basically, I can't think at all.

'C...Clara,' I just about manage to stutter. Our eyes meet and there is no doubt she's enjoying how the tables have turned. 'You don't have to do this.'

'I don't *have* to do anything for you,' she grins, having recovered surprisingly well from the ordeal I've put her through over the past half hour. Indeed, she looks bright-eyed and more alert than ever. I'd go as far as to say she's positively buzzing. 'But I *want* to do everything.'

And there she is again; that selfless girl who has looked after me tirelessly. She's put up with my bad moods and moments of bitter self-absorption. She's ferried me between home, hospitals, relatives and, during our down time, the beach. She's cooked and cleaned, and done way more than I wanted her to, not that I was in much of a position to assist. That's something that will change in the future though, if I can persuade her to stay with me. Not as my nurse, but as my partner...and my equal.

My breathing suddenly becomes sharp and ragged, as Clara pulls my remaining clothes away, exposing what even I consider to be an impressive erection. It's almost as though my body is trying to make up for lost time. I've never been small but the size of my cock tonight is verging on crazy.

'Oh wow,' murmurs Clara. As her breath ghosts across my delicate skin, I feel my cock jerk sharply in response, the ache verging on unbearable as a carnal sensation spreads throughout my entire abdomen. Almost immediately, she dips her head for a taste, and I am intimately aware of her warm soft hand moulding around my thickened girth, encouraging the head of my cock to be caressed by her warm, wet, eager tongue.

'Fuuuuuuuck!' I growl, low and deep, my desire utterly impossible to curtail. 'I need to be inside you.' So, so badly.

'No way. My turn,' she mutters, before returning her infinitely luxurious mouth back to me again.

I groan in hopeless submission, scooping my hand through Clara's soft hair to caress the back of her neck. This doesn't seem like the appropriate time to mention it, and actually, I couldn't construct a sentence right now if my life depended on it, but I am reminded of the most inappropriate question I jokingly asked Clara when we first met, which she handled so beautifully. She told me that information about how skilled she was at giving blow jobs was on a strictly need to know basis. But I'm in a perfect situation to answer that question now because I know. She's fucking amazing.

As her mouth continues to slide up and down my shaft with a perfect caress, her tongue providing an additional stimulation which is making my head spin, I think I understand why she's so talented. She isn't indulging in this activity simply as a form of repayment for the many climaxes I drove her to earlier. No. Going by the low moans regularly ascending from her throat, she's pleasuring me as much for her own enjoyment as mine. Although, thinking about it, that can't possibly be true because I am in heaven. Utter glorious heaven. To feel her lips moving down my shaft, her hand stroking my aching balls? Geez! If I die this very second, I will die the happiest man on earth.

'Please!' I cry out, mirroring the similar plea Clara made earlier, which of course I ignored. I'm not too proud to beg. I have to be inside her. But only when I sound like a truly desperate man, does she eventually relent.

'Should I be trying harder to keep your blood pressure down?' she teases.

'Yeah, screw my blood pressure. I've got more important things to focus on, because now you're in real trouble,' I groan, pulling her up the bed to join me. 'Are you ready?'

'I'm ready,' she replies, without even considering her answer.

With no time to waste, I reach across to my bedside drawer and pull out a condom. Ripping the wrapper, I swiftly roll it on, while Clara stares at me in disbelief. I send her a small, supportive smile, not least because I share her feelings. I can barely compute this is happening either, but I'm incredibly happy to confirm that it is.

Moving onto my knees, I settle myself between Clara's legs and lean over her open, wanton body. I hope that she can forgive me for being a little uncoordinated, as I get to grips with having sex for the first time after my accident. Silently, I send up a promise to improve if she'll stick with me.

'You still sure?' I feel the need to check one last time. Responding with a groan of exasperation, Clara wraps her feet around my back and pulls me close, guiding me into her. Helpless to resist, I sink slowly forwards, becoming utterly lost with every additional inch I disappear inside. She's incredibly tight, incredibly warm and incredibly slippery. Attempting to refocus when all around me reality is threatening to spin out of control, I glance down to see Clara's eyes are tightly closed, and the tendons in her neck raised. It seems impossible but I think she's about to orgasm again. She must have been a lot closer to the edge than I'd realised.

'Fuck!' Clara gasps, as I continue to slide deeper and deeper. 'Fuck! You're huge!'

'Do you want me to stop?' I murmur, through gritted teeth. Fuck only knows what I'll do if she says yes, because now I've tasted paradise, I'm not convinced I can bear to give it up.

'No! For fuck's sake, don't stop!' she replies, in a voice that is nothing like her own. Deep, gruff and strained, it sounds like she is using every ounce of available strength to hold herself together. And I admit to knowing exactly how she feels.

At last I bottom out. Holding still, I revel in the intense sensations of Clara's powerful muscles constricting and relaxing around me, as she attempts to get used to being filled so completely. It is agonisingly good to be enjoying a pleasure which I'd honestly feared might be lost to me. It's a relief, in every sense of the word. Except being with Clara of course, the pleasure hasn't just returned; it is already better than ever.

Gradually, my hips fall into an almost unbearably deliberate rhythm, purposefully smearing her clit against my groin, with the sole intention of maximising Clara's gratification. Gazing deeply into each other's eyes, our connection is deeply powerful as the enjoyment builds, even though we are scarcely moving. Never have I known such intimate sex; an acknowledgment that the slightest movement by your partner can send you crashing towards oblivion, with no prospect of being spared. Ever so gradually, I nudge Clara out to the very edge of her climax, just holding her there, with absolutely no intention of allowing her to fall. Potent and addictive, it's an experience I know I'll never get enough of.

'Let. Me. Come,' murmurs Clara, against my rough face. 'Fuck me...harder. I'm begging you.'

'Kiss me, and I'll think about it,' I reply, my lips already tumbling towards hers. As our warm tongues entwine, I do as Clara asks, safe in the knowledge that I will be following mere seconds behind her. It's half the reason I've been denying her release for so long. In my present, rather vulnerable state, I know I can't survive the intensity of one of Clara's climaxes.

Increasingly uninhibited, with ever-deepening strokes, I relish the impact of my pelvis clashing against hers. Clara groans into my mouth as her orgasm approaches fast. In a frenzied flurry of movement and sound, we are each responsible for the other's demise. Screaming out her uncontained joy, Clara's entire body spasms and twists, forcing me to drive even deeper inside. I can feel the ecstasy taking over my entire being as I close my eyes and allow natural instinct to guide me. At the very deepest point, just as Clara shatters for the final time, I explode, instantly overwhelmed by a sense of relief, delight and pure, unquestionable love.

EPILOGUE

CLARA

1 Year Later

FEELING SAFE, warm and loved, I very gradually regain consciousness after an excellent night's sleep. Without opening my eyes, I am vaguely aware of a gentle breeze flowing in through the partially open window, bringing with it the sweet melody of birdsong. Behind me, Brad tenderly starts to stroke my lower back and I groan encouragingly, pushing myself against him.

'Good morning,' I mutter contentedly, keeping my head on the pillow and my eyes tightly closed, just in case this all turns out to be the most fantastic dream in recorded history. It's certainly a risk, because if this isn't a dream it means I've ended up living with my soulmate and the sexiest guy I have ever known. Could I really be that lucky?

'Good morning, beautiful,' Brad replies, sounding equally content. Repositioning himself slightly, he kisses across my shoulders, as his wickedly capable hands start to wander. I'm not sure I've ever felt so loved, adored and utterly cherished as I do in this moment.

'Hey!' I pretend to complain. 'I thought sportsmen believed in abstaining before big events?'

'Mmmm, not this one,' he groans, his hands reaching forward to cup my breasts before gently squeezing the nipples. 'And certainly not when you're naked in my bed.'

Grinding my hips backwards, I moan and twist against him, silently urging Brad to continue. But I'm only partly joking. Today is a really big deal; the most prestigious race he's been involved in since his accident. Over the past year, this incredibly determined man has worked hard, particularly on his physio and mental recovery, to successfully return to the very top of his sport. And all that hard work has paid off. Indeed, his body now shows no visible signs that he suffered considerable injury just over a year ago.

Of course, I absolutely hate the thought of Brad being involved in a similar accident in the future, or something even worse, but I support him completely. Early on, I had to come to terms with the fact that racing cars is simply one aspect of the man I fell in love with. It's an integral part of his character. And, despite the dangers, I would no more attempt to change him than walk away from him.

I've attended every single one of Brad's races, to lend moral support. Occasionally we pass Henrietta in the VIP lounge which can lead to the situation becoming a little awkward. These days, she is far less inclined to be quite so effusive in her praise of me. We both silently acknowledge that I have captured the heart of the man she desired the most. But I try not to beat myself up about it too much. After all, it was Brad's decision in the long run; he was never going to return to her, whether anything happened with me or not.

Although I certainly can't blame Henrietta for being jealous; personally, I'd be livid. For not only is Brad the funniest, kindest most decent guy ever, but he is also a fucking wizard in bed. I have no idea how he continually makes me feel so good, but I'm certainly not going to question it. I just thank my lucky stars that it's him I get to enjoy carnal pleasures with every night...and some afternoons too. And the occasional morning. It is true that our sex life has evolved considerably since that first magical night we spent together; sometimes soft and gentle, on other occasions rampant and wild, but without fail always entirely loving.

'Mmmm,' he groans from behind, instantly snapping my attention back to the here and now. 'Do you know we've been together three hundred and eighteen days. I think we should celebrate in some way.'

'Is that number particularly relevant?' I giggle, knowing it isn't.

'Absolutely,' he confirms. 'That's three hundred and eighteen days that I consider myself to be just about the luckiest guy in the world.'

'You're very sweet,' I sigh, knowing that I'm the lucky one.

'As are you,' he replies with amusement. 'Not least because I do believe you have the most luscious, delectable, thoroughly edible arse in the whole of reality.'

And then, as though to prove his point, he places a line of scorching kisses down my spine, before sinking his teeth into one of my rounded cheeks. Already seriously turned on, I writhe upon the bedcovers, but am immediately distracted. Brad's hand is creeping forwards, over my hip, to edge between my legs. Tempting, teasing, the potential for mind-blowing stimulation is suggested but denied. I groan with frustration as his hand remains forever out of reach. The promise of so much more.

'But if you insist on me racing in a sexually frustrated state, then you're going to have to share that frustration with me.' I moan throatily in response. 'So, what's it going to be?' he queries playfully.

'Make me come,' I plead, my voice cracking slightly with desire. Instantly, Brad's fingers slide into the sticky mess and my hands automatically reach back towards him, to join in the fun.

'My pleasure, my love,' he murmurs against my ear. 'Always my pleasure.'

THE END

OUR TIME

FENELLA ASHWORTH

CHAPTER 1

ANNIE

For some reason, I glance at my watch yet again. It isn't as though checking it multiple times is going to slow down the inevitable passing of time and prevent me from being just as late as I originally feared. With one arm surreptitiously supporting my breasts and the other clasping my handbag, I race through the school grounds. Quite what convinced me to wear a low-cut bra today, rather than a more supportive option, I have no idea. But I can't deny that it's a decision I'm regretting enormously. It's not as though any lucky guy is going to get to see the little black, lacy number I randomly selected this morning, and the garment is clearly doing nothing for me. I definitely should have plumped for a more comfortable option.

Approaching the assembly hall, I slow to a walk, panting like some kind of asthmatic pervert. Geez, I'm depressingly unfit. Surely, a thirty second burst of jogging shouldn't have such a devastating effect on my respiratory system? Before I became a mum, I used to regularly sign up for charity runs. Sure, I wasn't particularly speedy, but I could do it. Pregnancy was a great excuse for me to stop all that fitness nonsense and I've been using the same excuse of having a child ever since. But it's an excuse which has been wearing thin for some time, given that Toby's now ten years old.

I take a couple of deep breaths and appreciate the warm May evening, before slipping inside the building.

'Mrs Peters,' the Headmistress almost immediately announces, before I've even stepped foot inside. I baulk slightly at her use of my married name, but given very few people have been informed our divorce is now finalised, I can hardly blame the woman.

'Mrs Smithson,' I reply cordially, my breathing still not entirely recovered.

'Please do come in and help yourself to refreshments.'

She points me towards a table laid out with tea, coffee, water and biscuits. I've always thought the only options they should offer at a parent-teacher evening are red, white and perhaps also shots. A glass of chilled wine is certainly exactly what I fancy right now. Unenthusiastically, I pour myself some water and glance around the room to get my bearings.

As is typical of these events, the large hall has been laid out with each subject teacher being assigned a table, positioned towards the outer edge of the room. The parents then mingle in the centre, approaching a teacher when they become available, to discuss the progress of their little darlings in the relevant subject area. The unexpected benefit of arriving late is that the initial surge of keen parents have departed, leaving a little more time and space for the rest of us. Not that I ever aimed to be late, of course. Tardiness is something I typically avoid as best I can. Unfortunately, with my dear parents on babysitting duty, I was obliged to wait for them to arrive. Then my dad started talking about the latest television series he'd got into and all hope was lost. But although their personalities do often make leaving on time a challenge, they couldn't be better grandparents. Utterly doting and in love with my son, I have no doubt Toby is currently being spoiled rotten. I don't doubt he'll already have talked them around to his way of thinking, masterminding the substitution of the healthy elements of his evening meal for the tub of chocolates I saw sticking out of my mother's handbag.

Toby's French teacher is just about to become available, so I loiter beside her table, glancing around for Lee. Unfortunately, it doesn't look as though my ex-husband has decided to turn up. Again. It's a worrying trend that is really starting to set in; a disinclination to be actively involved in our son's life. I can only hope it might reverse, sooner rather than later, or else I'm going to continue to feel guilty about my decision to split from him, for pretty much the rest of my life. In my defence, I was placed in an impossible situation, and although some women can deal with infidelity within the marriage, I'm afraid I'm not one of them.

'Anne!' Toby's French teacher exclaims, the smile on her face instantly mirrored by my own as I purposefully push away any negative thoughts. 'Do come and sit down.'

In between chatting with other parents and teachers, hers is the first of many glowing reports I receive that night. Although, I can't say I'm particularly surprised. I know I'm probably biased but Toby is an angel in my opinion, particularly when compared to some of his classmates who seem to act like the spawn of the Devil himself. At least, whenever they come around to play at our house anyway.

Not for the first time, I realise that being a mother is the most rewarding job I will ever do. To see your child grow up and learn, thanks to your input. To develop and mature because of the things you've taught him and the morals you've instilled within. It is quite an incredible thing.

Of course, there have been difficult times, although strangely I've found it much easier to cope since I became a single parent last year. Lee and I simply weren't working as a couple and I don't doubt that the strain was starting to show, particularly for Toby who had to put up with us constantly sniping at each other. It was a difficult decision to separate, but in my heart I know I've done the right thing. That's not to say that complications don't still exist. I do wonder if Lee is struggling to come to terms with our separation. I've done my best to ignore his poor parental support along with the string of inappropriate liaisons he's indulged in recently. I don't know if my ex is acting up or genuinely doesn't care so much about Toby now. I do know one thing, though; he is nothing like the man I married. In fact, I hardly recognise him at all these days, not that I dwell on that. All I can do is keep my energy focused on the one thing that really matters now; our son.

Well-meaning friends and family members occasionally suggest that I might consider starting to date again but, in all honesty, online dating sounds like a complete nightmare and one which I have no intention of subjecting myself to. Besides, there have been so few men that I've ever truly desired. It would take somebody extraordinary to fit into our lives now and Toby and I are doing just fine as we are. I try not to think too far ahead, when my precious baby is old enough to fly the nest, or go to university. For now, I'm content to live in the moment. I have to be.

Dragging my attention back to the task in hand, I glance at Toby's most recent report card. Against the odds, I've managed to see almost all of his teachers. Only two remain. Mr Abbot, the science teacher, and Mr Harrison, Toby's new Geography teacher. Science is obviously a subject which invokes lengthy discussions, because the queue around that table remains considerable. I therefore take the decision to go in search of the famous Mr Geography; he's a new addition to the teaching staff that I haven't met yet. However, I do know he's already become quite a hit with the students, particularly my own son, if the stories he's been coming home with recently are anything to go by.

It doesn't take me long to track Mr Harrison down, but if I'd known what lay in store for me, I'd definitely have taken some time to compose myself. As my eyes rest on Toby's Geography teacher, I'm conscious of doing a double take, my mouth unattractively hanging open in shock. For there, seated before me, is the adult version of a friend I'd once known incredibly well. He's filled out substantially, but is still easily recognisable as the guy I spent many of my teenage years lusting over. With a well-muscled, broad chest, powerful arms visible beneath his short-sleeved shirt and ruggedly handsome good looks, he remains seriously fit. No, for once let me be completely honest; he's *fucking* gorgeous. How is it that men only become more handsome with age? Effortlessly so it seems to me, growing into their skins in a way that women can only admire. And in some cases envy. Jack is breathtaking in the literal sense of the word, for I am physically struggling to draw enough oxygen into my heaving lungs.

Unsurprisingly, it doesn't take him long to realise he's attracting rapt attention from a panting bystander.

'Annie?' he mutters incredulously, his voice instantly recognisable to me, like a long-forgotten, ancient melody. Placing his hands on the table, Jack rises to his feet to tower over me, his expression the mirror image of my own. 'My God! Is that really you?'

Just standing there, I can feel the years rolling back. I could almost be seventeen again, although I guess at the ripe old age of thirty-eight, I'm not entirely past it. Not yet anyway. The strange thing is that I haven't been called Annie by anyone other than my closest family for years. Since attending university, I've always just been Anne to strangers and acquaintances. But then, I guess, Jack doesn't fall into either of those two categories. Certainly, once upon a time, he knew me better than any other person alive.

'Yes,' I just about manage to squeak, dismayed at how breathless my voice sounds.

'It must be twenty years since we last met?' It's rather disconcerting that neither of us can tear our eyes away from each other.

'Yeah...twenty,' I agree, conversational repartee clearly not operating at full throttle. Although to be fair, I have just experienced one hell of a shock.

For Jack wasn't just *a* guy in my past. He was *the* guy. My first love. And I've been subconsciously comparing all other men to him ever since, very unsuccessfully as it happens. Not that anything ever developed between us at school, worst luck. My love was the silent, brooding kind, although no less potent for being so.

'I thought you'd moved away,' I stutter, managing to find my tongue at last. It isn't the best conversation starter, but trust me, it could have been a hundred times worse.

The truth is, I'd kept tabs on him as best I could for the first several years. Our parents had drifted in the same social circles back then, so it wasn't difficult to gain snippets of information from here and there, about the guy I'd always desired. But life goes on. Times change. And even the snippets eventually faded to nothing and all contact was lost.

With the rise of social media, like so many before me, I had taken the opportunity to look up any exes, largely in the hope that they'd been at least marginally less successful after we'd split. Not that I'd wished that upon Jack, of course, although that was probably because we'd never been in a relationship. But for Jack, there had been no available information. It was almost as though he'd disappeared off the face of the planet. An imaginary friend from my childhood. My secret unrequited love. And now, suddenly, here he is in the flesh, taking away my ability to think as effortlessly as he'd always done.

'You're a teacher?' I know. It isn't a particularly perceptive observation given I'm at my son's school, and he's wearing a name badge that announces he teaches Geography.

'And you're a mother?' he replies. I can't quite work out if there's sadness in his tone, or pride, but there is definitely something.

'Yes,' I confirm. He waves his hand towards the empty chair opposite him. 'Toby Peters.' Appreciatively, I sit, grateful to be taking the weight from my shaking legs. They'd been feeling increasingly unsteady ever since running into Jack, and were failing fast.

'Ah, I should have known,' he smiled broadly, instantly displaying the dimples I remember from my childhood. 'A charming boy. So full of kindness and intelligence.'

And now I can't help but grin goofily back at Jack. It's my natural reaction when anybody praises my son. But coming from the lips of the man whose opinion I once sought above all others, it is praise indeed.

'Thank you, Mr Harrison,' I stumble, quickly regretting the use of his surname. I'm not entirely sure why I call Jack that. It must be the unexpected situation we find ourselves in.

'I think we can dispense with the formalities, don't you?' he suggests, smiling kindly. 'After all, we do have quite a history together.'

Somehow, his statement makes our past sound far more illicit than it actually was. But far from being embarrassed, I feel only the thrill of the chase.

CHAPTER 2

JACK

S hit. I can't believe Annie Appleby is sitting right in front of me, after so much time has passed. My mind has gone completely blank and I'm horribly aware of fumbling hopelessly around the edges of our conversation, making random, incredibly awkward statements. I honestly wouldn't be surprised to discover that I'm blushing, and it's taking all of my concentration to look her directly in the eyes. For fuck's sake. What am I? Eighteen again? I literally can't believe she's here.

Swallowing, I take a deep breath and try to gain control of my thoughts. But it's a struggle. The truth is, I always lose a little confidence in the presence of a beautiful woman, and there's no denying that Annie has grown into one of those. I can still see the girl I adored in my earlier years, but there's a maturity to her now. A poise and confidence that naturally accompanies life experience. The most stark difference in Annie is her hair. The last time I saw her it was dyed green for some event or other she was attending; a charity run, I believe. It's mousy brown now. Long. It suits her. But equally, I secretly hope the spirit she once had, hasn't been eaten up with the day to day grind of daily life, love and responsibilities. I swallow again; she literally has me salivating.

Continuing to admire, I can see that her skin is as flawless as ever. Her smile draws me in, her perfectly aligned teeth, and those lips... Lips that I spent far too many years dreaming about kissing when I was a younger man. But it was not meant to be.

I'm vaguely aware that the hall is still full of people, but there is only one person I want to speak to. Only one person I need to be close to. And right now, it's taking every ounce of focus I have, not to reach across the table and touch her. Stroke her hand. Pull her into a hug. At this moment, I don't actually care. I just want to be near her again.

Unexpectedly, I'm reminded of an occasion I haven't thought about for the longest time. We were at some kind of party during our youth with a bunch of other kids; I don't remember where. Beneath a starry sky, Annie and I were sitting side by side around a campfire, staring into the flames. Thanks to sharing a blanket which was wrapped around both of our shoulders, I was forced to snuggle up tight to her. It felt incredibly intimate. There were plenty of other people around us, but at the time, it felt as though it was just the two of us. Only one person had mattered to me that night; the rest of humanity were meaningless faces in comparison.

When I was younger, I'd replayed that scene a thousand times in my imagination, knowing I should have stepped up and dared to tell Annie how I felt. Of course, she could have said something too, if she'd really been interested in me. But, thanks to my inability to be courageous and admit my feelings, I'd let everything slide. In silence, I'd continued to adore from afar until the inevitable happened. Undoubtedly fed up of waiting for me to make a move, when she was approached by another guy at school, she agreed to go on a date with him. He was her first real boyfriend and it literally killed me, every time I saw them together. For six months, I festered in silence until the pain became too damn much to take. At which point, I did the gentlemanly thing and backed away, displaying the kind of morals my parents had always instilled in me. Indeed, I backed so far away that I went to university across the other side of the globe, where the vision of them together couldn't torment me any longer. The next time I'd heard any news about Annie, years later, it was to discover that she'd got married.

My poor choices had lost me the single woman I'd always desired. And given my chance again, I'm not entirely confident that I'd act with such decency. Should I have stayed and fought for her? In my heart, I already know what the answer is; damn right I should have done. I've always been very proud of my morals. However, after a string of failed relationships, I have learnt the hard way and I appreciate the value of discovering your soulmate. That unlikely, million to one chance of finding the person that makes your heart sing. It is something I would grab with both hands now, should I ever be so lucky to encounter it again. When we were eighteen, I didn't believe it was our time. But I was too immature to realise that time may never come around again.

Realising that I'm staring, I try to look away but it's impossible. Instead, I make a further attempt to converse, hoping to do a better job of it this time around.

'Well, as I'm sure you can imagine, Toby is a complete joy to teach.' Instantly, I'm dazzled by her immense pride; Annie literally lights up from the inside whenever her son is mentioned. And quite rightly so; he's an amazing little boy. Unlike some of the complete shits in that class. Believe me, if all the children were like Toby Peters, my job here would be a breeze.

Automatically without thinking, I glance down at the ring finger on her left hand. I'm surprised by the blast of elation I feel, to note that no wedding band resides there. I know I shouldn't read too much into that, particularly not these days. I mean, some unmarried women wear jewellery on every finger, while some married women wear no rings at all. But although my logical mind is capable of reasoning and deduction, it seems my heart does not wish to be persuaded.

'He's smart, quick-thinking and really engaged,' I continue with a gentle smile, trying to pull my thoughts back on track. 'But I'm not telling you anything you don't already know, am I? So, tell me. How have you been?'

'Oh...good. Thank you.' Annie's acting as though somebody

checking in on her and asking about her wellbeing isn't the norm. 'And you?'

'Yeah, same thanks,' I reply with a nod. I get the impression that we're both being equally untruthful with each other. As far as I can tell, we look like two people who are both in search of happiness. But not one to linger on my single, relatively lonely status, I continue. 'And how are your parents?'

I've always had a soft spot for Alice and Sam. As a child, I spent many happy hours hanging around their house. Their garden was perfect for messing about in and climbing trees with Annie, and without fail, their cupboards were always far better stocked than at home. My own parents always preferred fruit over chocolate; an unfathomable state of affairs which the younger version of me could never quite comprehend.

'They're on excellent form, thank you,' she grins, looking genuinely happy for the first time since she arrived. 'On babysitting duty tonight.'

'Ah, yes. Of course.' I respond as though this information is unsurprising, but the truth of the matter is, my interest is piqued. So Annie doesn't have a significant other at home, then? Suddenly, I find myself dying to ask about Toby's father and discover more. But I'm spared the need for doing so because at that moment, a tall, dark-haired, whippet-like man marches towards the table and sits down beside Annie without any introduction.

'Sorry I'm late,' he mutters, not particularly sounding it.

My chest immediately constricts, the answer to my question provided without the inconvenience of words. I watch Annie's face as she turns to glance at the man, a sharp, questioning look in her eyes. After a short pause, she turns to face me again and I attempt to convey an expression which doesn't illustrate the depth of my disappointment. Annie looks unsettled and surprised. Perhaps it's the pressure of having her current partner and an old friend in such close proximity to each other. The apprehension of past meeting present, and not knowing what might come out of that conversation. Introductions are swiftly made, breaking the growing silence.

'This is Toby's Geography teacher, Jack,' explains Annie. 'Jack, this is Toby's father Lee.'

I watch for a second as the man weighs me up. A curious look flashes across his face, no doubt due to Annie's informal use of my first name. On my part, I attempt to suppress the feeling of pain I'm experiencing, on realising that my assumption about this man was correct; they are partners. Fuck it. But both of our good manners are quick to reassert and we briefly shake hands across the table.

'Very pleased to meet you,' I mutter, even though I'm sure the sentiment is not mirrored in my tone.

'Likewise,' he answers, gruffly.

Annie is sitting very upright now, her hands clenched in her lap as though she's having to purposefully steady herself. I don't pretend to understand what's going on between the two of them but their body language is far from warm. That, in itself, is a blessing. I couldn't cope with seeing another man's hands or lips on her, particularly not so soon after discovering she's apparently back in my life, given I'm going to be teaching her son.

Things are obviously not rosy at home between them, but perhaps they just had a row this morning. It really isn't my business to pry into someone else's marital life. Stifling a sigh, I repeat the praise I have for Toby, doing my best to focus entirely upon Lee. I find it minimises the sharp stab of pain in my gut which I feel every time I glance at Annie. As I talk, I continue to observe them closely. There is no emotional intimacy between them at all, but that's how some marriages become, isn't it? I wouldn't know from experience, having never been married. I got close once, but it was not to be. But I do know that a fairy-tale relationship is very rare. For Annie's sake, I wish that wasn't true, although how likely is it to find a single person you are entirely happy with? Someone you desire completely?

I do feel a sadness on Annie's behalf though. In my memories, she's always existed as a vibrant spirit, so full of life. Amused by the ridiculous, she has the most amazing laugh. Sometimes when we were kids, we'd start giggling, only to find ourselves unable to stop. Annie's mirth would eventually turn into a combination of cackling, snorting and hiccupping, as tears poured down our faces. Just thinking about it now, I have to force myself not to smile. It's an invaluable core memory that I've carried around with me for decades. Dismayed to discover that girl might no longer exist in this world, a flash of sorrow passes through me. The Annie here today doesn't look like she's laughed out of control for longer than she can remember. Actually, I've never seen her look so defeated. I only wish I could do something to resolve it.

CHAPTER 3

JACK

For the remainder of the week after seeing Annie and her husband, I feel rather emotionally wrung-out. By the time the weekend arrives, I decide to give myself a stern talking to, in the only way I know how; a circular thirteen mile run. Thirteen might be unlucky for some, but it is one of my favourite routes, taking me off-road to enjoy some of the beautiful countryside that surrounds the quiet town in which I live. Plus, I always feel a great sense of well-being after completing what equates to a half-marathon.

I leave home crazy early that morning, just as the sun is starting to rise, locking my house up behind me. It's a pleasant, four bedroom detached property located in a quiet cul-de-sac, not far from the school. My situation isn't what I'd dreamt of growing up, given I'd always wanted a family. But life happens, I guess. Unfortunately, I've always had a knack for choosing the wrong woman. Or in Annie's case, backing down when I should have stepped up. Although my consistent failure didn't really start to show as a trend until my late twenties.

I'd sailed through life until that point assuming I just wasn't meeting the right kind of girl, but ultimately, I had to acknowledge it was more than that. Each of my girlfriends was never quite what I expected or needed from a life partner. Looking back now with a little perspective, I'm pretty sure the issue stems from my friendship with Annie. We were so close. We shared pretty much everything, with the exception of my true feelings for her, of course. I guess there aren't many women in this world who can match up to your childhood expectations of the partner you want to be with, when the template you're using is your best friend.

Taking a well-trodden path across a large open field, the sound of birdsong filling my senses, my feet rhythmically hit the ground as I try to console myself. Logically analysing the situation, I have to admit that if Annie and I had got together as teenagers, the relationship probably wouldn't have lasted. Who knows? Maybe we would have been childhood sweethearts, got married young and had a bunch of kids by now. It was statistically most unlikely, although it did occasionally happen. But the truth of the matter was, Annie had been placed on a pedestal early in my life and other women would always struggle to compare. The real-life Annie probably couldn't even compare to the dream version, for that's what it was; a dream.

I run at a solid pace without pausing to catch my breath. By the time my home is edging back into sight, I feel invigorated, refreshed and ready to take on the world. Exercise is always a great generator of those feel-good endorphins and I certainly need some of those on my side right now. Unfortunately, despite my emotional high, I'm still not sure how I should approach the Annie situation, even though I've steadily pondered it for the last thirteen miles. Should I back away again, even though I can see she's unhappy with this Lee character, or should I stand up and fight for the woman that I've always loved? In my heart, the decision is easy; I fight. But then that damn moral compass of mine swings back into life; she's in a relationship and I should do the right thing. But the question is, what is the right thing? Long term, perhaps the right thing is to help Annie out of the situation she's in, and remind her of what it feels like to laugh until you cry.

I SPEND much of that weekend in my garden. The weather is glorious and the sunshine feels so good against my skin, particularly when I know I'll be stuck inside classrooms again tomorrow. Having tended to the vegetables I'm attempting to grow, I experience an unexpected urge for a freshly made ham salad sandwich for lunch, using some of the tomatoes and green leaves I've grown. Just one problem though. The only bread I have is a few days old, and this creation will definitely require something freshly cooked from the bakery down the road.

Having scrubbed the dirt from my hands as best I can, I grab my wallet and stroll down to the local shops. As I stand in a short queue, I realise that if I wasn't a teacher, I'd probably have to work in a bakery. The smell alone must be enough to ensure that all their staff are permanently happy. Well, maybe not, but it certainly does it for me. Afterwards, I walk back across the park towards home, intermittently opening the paper bag and inhaling deeply. Nothing beats a fresh loaf. Suddenly, I hear my name being shouted from across the park and look for the source.

'Mr Harrison!'

Ah, I retract my last statement. There is something that hands down beats a fresh loaf of bread.

'Mr Harrison! Over here!'

Ignoring his shushing mother, Toby is bouncing up and down on a picnic rug, Annie sitting beside him looking wildly embarrassed by her son's behaviour. With a broad grin, I lope towards them, noting a range of food laid out on an adjacent rug; sandwiches, crisps, fruit, sausages, pork pies and cartons of fresh juice. They are clearly just about to indulge in a picnic lunch and I have to say, it looks amazing. At the last second, Toby breaks free of his mother's clutches and bounces over to greet me.

'Hi there, Tobe!' I say. 'Wow! What an incredible picnic!'

'Sit down and join us,' offers Toby, practically jumping up and down with excitement at my arrival. I glance over his head towards Annie and for a second, our eyes meet. I feel a sharp jolt in my abdomen in response to the intensity of her gaze, but any meaning is indecipherable.

'Oh well, surely you're spending time with your Mummy, aren't you?' I explain, remembering that trying to gently refuse a highly excitable ten year old is an almost impossible feat.

'She won't mind! Come and meet her!'

'Actually, we've already met at parents' evening,' I attempt to explain, while being dragged towards the picnic blanket by my hand. 'Hello,' I add to Annie, as I arrive at her location.

'Hello.' Her smile is gentle and kind. Just like the woman herself.

'Mummy always makes *way* too much food! Sit with us?' Over Toby's head, I glance questioningly towards Annie. I don't want to intrude on the precious alone time with her son, but equally, I'm not stupid enough to pass on an opportunity to spend time with them both.

'It's fine,' she says soothingly. 'It would be a pleasure if you could join us.'

'Very well,' I agree, dropping to one corner of the blanket amid cheering from Toby. 'But if you want me to clear off at any time, please just say so. I won't take offence.'

The next hour of my life is one of the happiest I can remember in the longest time. The food is delicious and the company even more so. I discover that I adore watching Annie and Toby interact, for they have such a close relationship. It sounds obvious for a mother and son to naturally be that way, but it isn't always the case, at least not in my teaching experience anyway. The only difficult part is remembering to physically keep my distance. Because the truth is, all I really want to do is take Annie into my arms and hold her.

Just then, a sound rings through the warm air, guaranteed to grab and hold the attention of any child within a one mile radius; the chimes of an approaching ice cream van. Toby is instantly on his feet, all thought of the strawberries he'd been enjoying, instantly forgotten.

'Ooooh! Mummy! Can I? Can I?' he chatters excitedly.

'Yes,' sighs a resigned Annie, reaching for her handbag. But before she has a chance to complete the transaction, I lean towards her and place my hand over hers.

'Please, allow me.'

Our bodies unite for the first time in so many years and something inside me ignites. I've always scoffed at people who suggest a chemical reaction can be caused by the touch of another's hand but in that moment, I encounter it for real. An explosion of unrestrained desire crackles its way up my arm, along my neck and straight into the base of my skull. And by the looks of Annie's astonished, wide-eyed expression, something pretty similar has happened to her too. My touch seems to still us both, for we don't move for several seconds. Toby soon becomes restless though, helping to break the connection we'd been sharing.

'Perhaps you'll buy us one each?' I suggest, pulling the wallet from my pocket and handing a ten pound note across to Toby. 'It's the very least I can do, to thank you for letting me share this wonderful picnic.'

'Cool! Thanks Mr Harrison!'

We both sit in silence, watching Toby race across the grass in excitement towards the ice cream van, feeling grown up for being allowed to make his purchase alone, like an adult. Why do children want to grow up so fast? I can remember feeling exactly the same way myself whereas now, in retrospect, I'd give pretty much anything to get those years back again. Children simply have no idea of the sheer enjoyment and freedom of childhood. I suppose, like anything, only when you're far removed from it, can one look back at those halcyon days and recognise that truly was the time of your life. I certainly feel that way about my own childhood and consequently about the woman who currently sits beside me.

Glancing across at Annie again, I can't help but notice she's continuing to hold the back of her hand where I touched it seconds earlier. Her subconscious reaction emboldens me. I know I should learn to hold my tongue, but where Annie is concerned, that is a physical impossibility. She makes me feel alive, confident, courageous and brave. So although I should probably exercise caution, caution is the last thing that's on my mind right now.

'Your husband isn't with you today?'

'No, no he isn't,' she admits. I can see her wavering about saying more so, instead of making polite conversation to fill any uncomfortable gaps which might arise, I hold my nerve and remain silent. 'He's also not my husband,' she explains at last. 'We separated last year.'

A blast of adrenaline fills my body and I check myself, fighting hard to suppress my elation at this news. After all, the breakdown of a marriage is hardly a cause for celebration, particularly when a child is involved.

'I'm sorry to hear that,' I reply. And I genuinely am, if only for the pain the situation undoubtedly caused her and Toby.

'Are you really? Truthfully?' Annie queries, a small smile lifting the edges of her mouth. She knows me better than I know myself.

'Honestly? I'm probably not as sorry as I ought to be.'

CHAPTER 4

ANNIE

Glancing across at Jack, I can see emotions of relief crossing his face. I'm reminded of his dismayed expression at parents' evening, when I introduced him to Lee. Open honesty is one of the many things I've always adored about Jack; it is certainly a welcome change from the insular, secretive behaviour of my ex-husband. But comparing the two men is wildly unfair to Lee. Briefly, I wonder whether my unreasonable expectations assisted in our marriage breakdown. Sadly, I'm forced to conclude that, as much as I'd like to entirely blame my ex for his duplicitous ways, our failure was a joint one. I just hope Jack understands why I haven't mentioned Lee's status before now. Ideally, I'd have said something the second he joined us today, but I could never have raised the subject in front of Toby; the matter is still too sensitive and painful for him.

'May I see you again soon?' Jack suddenly blurts out. 'Can we have a drink together? Oh God, that sounds so lame!' His admission instantly causes me to giggle. I feel so lighthearted and happy, not least because I'm getting the distinct impression that Jack might be interested in me. And I can scarcely deny the feeling is entirely recip-rocated.

He's in casual clothes today and I've been struggling to keep my eyes off him as I visually consume every inch of his spectacular body. Thanks to the warm spring weather, he's wearing shorts which display his well-muscled legs to perfection, and an open-necked shirt that hints of a mildly hairy chest that I'd love to discover more of. Sporting some weekend stubble on his face, I honestly don't think he's ever looked more desirable. I know that no-one in the world is perfect but right now, from this close-up vantage point, Jack is ticking every possible box.

'Don't laugh at me,' he complains playfully. 'I'm trying to navigate the social constraints that you and I rarely operated under as kids.'

'So then don't,' I suggest, accompanying my challenge with a raised eyebrow and a cheeky smile. 'Just say what you feel and we'll take it from there.'

'What I feel?' he repeated. Obviously amused, he considers this for a moment. 'You don't want to know what I feel, Annie.'

'Try me.' I'm biting the inside of my lip, in an attempt to stop the enormous goofy grin which is threatening to take over my face. Now I remember how I loved playing with this guy; our banter has always been superb.

'No way.'

'What have you got to lose?' I smirk.

'You. Again,' he admits seriously. Instantly, all hilarity seeps away, leaving me rapt with anticipation, my pulse beating steadily in my ears.

'And what if your words do the very opposite of lose me? What if they make me want you even more?' I stutter, every cell in my body entirely focused on his response.

'Annie,' Jack instantly growls, his timbre deeper than I've ever heard. 'Don't tease me.'

'You can be brave...or not. It's up to you,' I explain, sending him a small but hopeful smile. 'But I think we're fundamentally still the same people we were twenty years ago. Somewhere inside, I'm certainly the playful, cheeky girl I used to be, even though I have precious little chance to demonstrate it these days. And I don't think you've changed much either. That's the only reason I'm daring to speak to you in this way.'

'Very well,' he says. Both of us pause and glance towards the ice cream van. I need to ensure Toby remains at a suitable distance away, so as not to hear any wicked admissions that Jack might be planning to make. At least, I bloody well hope he's planning them.

'Yes?' I reply, surprised to find myself panting lightly. I am literally on tenterhooks, awaiting an insight about how Jack truly feels.

Unexpectedly, he leans towards me, just inches from my personal space, and lowers his voice accordingly.

'I want to make love to you, Annie,' he growls.

Yes! I want to punch the air and celebrate but instead, all I can do is stare into his azure-blue eyes, blushing and utterly speechless. Jack pauses, studying me carefully, no doubt calculating whether he should continue or not. But having apparently received no negative feedback, he decides to chance it.

' I want to sink myself inside you...deeper than you've ever experienced before. And pretty much remain there until the end of time.' His confession ends with a low moan, as though it's taking all of his self-control not to act upon his desires.

I can feel the heat radiating from my cheeks, along with a smile I simply can't contain.

'Is that what you wanted to hear?' he asks, with a strangled laugh.

'That will certainly do for starters,' I confirm.

'In which case, I think you owe me. My request that we go out for a drink has just been upgraded,' he explains, looking delighted by my response. 'Will you accompany me to dinner one evening?'

'I'll consider it...'

'Well, consider it fast,' Jack suggests. 'Your son is on his way back.'

'In that case, fuck yeah!'

Thanks to my wildly unexpected response, by the time poor Toby returns to us, it is to find his mother and his Geography teacher cackling wildly and looking extremely pleased with themselves.

'What's going on?' he complains, thrusting an ice cream into each of our hands, before digging into the pocket of his shorts and passing Jack the change.

'Sorry, Sweetheart,' I reply, sending him a soft smile. 'Just being silly.'

For a while we all sit together, enjoying our ice creams and chatting away. But what Jack dared to admit earlier has changed the entire tone between us. And as much as I adore my son, part of me does wish he wasn't sitting between us on the picnic blanket right now, acting like a conversational contraceptive.

'So, why a teacher?' I ask Jack, in an attempt to continue the flow of conversation and steer us away from any inappropriate or risqué subjects. 'I thought you wanted to go into finance?'

'Yeah, I did once upon a time, but I guess life aspirations change,' shrugs Jack. 'When I was abroad, I undertook some charity work building schools in rural African communities, staying on to teach for a while. I admit I kind of fell into teaching, but it's become the natural fit for me. There's no other job I'd rather do now.'

'Well, you must be very good at it. My son has nothing but praise for you!'

'Mu-um,' complains Toby, looking up from his mobile phone to send me a look I'm familiar with. 'Don't be so embarrassing!'

'I'm not,' I giggle, feeling very lighthearted. 'I'm just explaining to Mr Harrison how he's definitely in the top five list of your favourite teachers!'

'Well, if that's true, I'm very honoured,' grins Jack, making me want to kiss him. 'Thank you.'

The truth is, he fascinates me. I find myself wanting to know everything about him...to discover all of his secrets, although I recognise this might not be the most appropriate opportunity to do so.

'And how about you? What do you do for work?' Jack asks.

'For a while, I worked in the field of scientific research,' I admit. 'But right now, I'm pulling together a publication on the various findings we helped to uncover.' Like many parents before me, I've discovered that it isn't easy to hang on to a well-paid, full-time job when you are suddenly responsible for every school run and all the school holiday childcare. For reasons I assume are linked with his social life, Lee has only been willing to have Toby to stay with him every other weekend. The impact such constraints have on my job proves that single parenting isn't all it's cracked up to be.

'Wow,' breathes Jack, clearly impressed. 'But then you always were the brainbox.'

Grabbing his mobile phone, Jack then makes an obvious display of flicking through the various screens, before turning to face me with a grin.

'Do you think I could borrow your phone please, Annie? Mine seems to have run out of battery and there's an urgent text I need to send.'

'Sure,' I chuckle, unlocking my own and passing it across. Jack's as easy to read as my own child and I can see he's up to mischief of some sort. No doubt, I'll find out what kind very soon. After much button clicking, the device is returned to me.

'Thanks,' he says, sending me the naughtiest grin I've ever had the pleasure to receive.

'You're very welcome.'

'Am I?' he mouths playfully, firstly ensuring Toby's attention is elsewhere.

Just then, my own phone buzzes, confirming the arrival of a new message. Glancing at it quizzically, I discover the text is from a newly created contact in my address book called "For God's sake call me soon, please". Sending Jack a quizzical look, largely because I have no doubt he's the instigator, I scroll through and read the message.

"I KNOW what I said before Toby returned, and that still stands. But the truth of the matter is, I just want to spend time with you, Annie. I want to take you out to dinner. I want to talk to you. And I'd love for us to get to know each other again. I do physically desire you but my mental desire is even stronger. Please let me know when you're free? I want to see you again as soon as possible x"

. . .

Touched by his sentiment, I glance wordlessly across at Jack, only to discover him staring back at me intensely, desire pouring from his eyes. I swallow hard and blink away the threatening tears. Fortunately, or not, our moment is disturbed by Toby.

'Please can I go and play on the climbing frames, Mum?' he asks. I glance across at the playground, assessing the distance. He'll be too far away for me to comfortably remain seated here, so I'll need to join him.

'Yes, of course,' I reply. 'I'll just pack up the picnic and be over. You go on ahead.'

'Thanks, Mum!' he grins, sprinting away from the relative shade we're seated in, to frolic in the sunshine.

In silence, Jack remains with me to assist in tidying away the picnic. Only when the blanket has been folded neatly and placed at the top of my bag do we finally face each other.

'I just need to say this, before I lose my nerve,' he says, his words unusually rushed for a man typically so confident. 'I adore you, Annie.'

I swallow hard, gazing up at his face in astonishment. I want to admit that the feeling is completely mutual, but he's already started to talk again.

'I always have done, and I always will do. And on that note, before I embarrass myself any further, I should leave. Thank you for the delicious picnic and a most enjoyable afternoon.'

And with that, he scoops up my right hand, sending all manner of flutterings through every part of my body as he does so, and places a tender kiss onto my palm. His lips are soft and moist as they move across my sensitive skin, instantly making my pussy throb urgently in response. I want this man. Fuck, do I want him.

'Goodbye, Annie.'

'Goodbye, Jack,' I whisper, not confident that I'll ever discover my voice again.

CHAPTER 5

JACK

A grand total of five days have passed since Annie and I last set eyes on each other and, I don't know about her, but I've been going crazy with desire. Literally, the first thing I see in the morning, before I even open my eyes, is Annie's smiling face. The same at night; she's the last thing I see. It is taking a continued effort to concentrate on my classes too. To say I can't wait for Saturday evening is a major understatement. And then, all of a sudden, time speeds up and our first date is upon us. Of course, that isn't entirely true. In the past, as kids, we'd accompanied each other to hundreds of events and parties. Annie was quite literally my "plus one" throughout my entire adolescence. But it never felt like *this*.

As agreed through a number of texts we've exchanged during the week, I've booked a table at an out-of-town restaurant with excellent reviews. We'd previously debated about whether we should dine locally but, in the end, decided we'd rather not be overlooked by friends, acquaintances or school parents. We both want to give this thing a chance, not potentially allow someone's thoughtless comments to spoil it at the last hurdle. And the best part is, we've got the whole evening free. Although I understand Lee's generally being a bit of a pain in the arse about spending time with his son, Toby is scheduled to stay with his father for the entire weekend. Not that I'm making any assumptions but, if things go well, I don't necessarily have to say goodbye to Annie later, only goodnight. Instantly, I feel a deep ache in my groin, just from the thought of it.

I pick Annie up at her home that evening. My natural instinct is to pull her into my arms and kiss her, but instead, I simply open the car door. I sense that she's nervous too. Almost as though we are both taking baby-steps, neither of us wishing to screw up what could be. Our conversation during the journey is relaxed, although I notice that the topics discussed are all very safe ones; school, Toby, the weather and a couple of items which have been reported on the news. But that's fine. I'd rather wait until I can give Annie my full attention, to cover more important subjects.

We spend the evening seated at an intimate table for two by the window. The wide, sweeping views outside are incredible; immaculately-maintained gardens which run onto rolling fields, all beneath a gradually setting, orange sun. But to be honest, it's the view inside the building which has me transfixed. In a floral dress, with her hair piled upon her head, Annie literally takes my breath away, each and every time I glance at her.

The meal we enjoy is excellent although, to be honest, I hardly taste it. I'm spellbound by Annie, just like her entire focus has been on me all evening. And it's thrilling. Completely thrilling. Our bodies are speaking to each other in a way that words never can, our souls conversing directly. I have no doubt that, the moment we're in private, we will no longer be able to resist the inevitable. But here in public view, we are managing to maintain our distance.

That is until I can bear it no longer. My fingers are literally tingling with a desire to touch her, hold her, pleasure her. Very slowly, my hand creeps to the centre of the table. I edge the coffee cups and flickering candle that separates us to one side, and dare to slide my fingers towards hers. In an almost reflex reaction, she quickly takes my hand, a red flush appearing on her face when she does so. As we stare deeply into each other's eyes, she rolls her bottom lip between her teeth. My God. How I wish it was me providing that stimulation, not Annie herself.

Gradually, the smiles we share grow into great big cheesy grins. I feel happy. Happier than I can ever remember. I'm just so damn proud to be seen in her company, so lighthearted, young and free again. Nothing can compare to this high. And then an awareness creeps over me. How being with some people can drain you and grind you down, whereas others have the ability to boost your sense of wellbeing and elevate you in every way. For me, Annie has always fallen into the latter category.

Still holding her hand, my thumb starts to stroke the soft, fleshy underside of her thumb. Only then does she unexpectedly pull away. I retract my hand and gaze at her quizzically. Have I just completely misread the situation?

'What's up?' I ask cautiously.

'I don't know if I can do this.'

'Do what?'

'I don't know if I can risk being rejected by you...again,' she adds in a voice so quiet that I can scarcely pick out the word. For a short while I study her carefully but say nothing, largely because I'm not sure of the best way to proceed. The last thing I want to do is spoil our evening by sounding accusatory, but I know exactly which incident she's referring to, and I don't think Annie is being entirely fair.

'You can't reject somebody who isn't free to give themselves to you,' I state, gently but firmly. I remember the occasion as though it happened only yesterday. I'd been eighteen and it was a few months before I cleared off abroad. A group of us had all gone to a party and Annie had attended with one of my mates; they'd been dating for a few months by that point. She'd come onto me pretty strong that night. There had been no double meaning to her words when she'd explicitly stated that she fancied me. I don't doubt she was pissed because it was so completely out of character for her. At least, I hope she was drunk, because otherwise I would have lost some respect for her that night. Having zero interest in cheating myself, I have never had any time for those willing to do so within a relationship.

'I'm sorry?'

'You're referring to the night of Jake Thompson's party?'

'Oh...I'm really surprised you remember that,' she admits, looking ashamed.

'Are you kidding me?' I murmur. Like I'm ever going to forget the one time the woman I desire more than life itself comes onto me...and I turn her away?

'I declared my hand that night,' she recalls sadly. 'Pretty much threw myself at you.'

'You were drunk.'

'I *was* drunk,' she admits. '*Very* drunk. But to be honest, I'd never have had the courage to admit my true feelings sober. And you rejected me. Very nicely. Very kindly. But it was a rejection all the same.'

'I had to. You were with someone else...'

'But he never meant a fraction of what you did to me. I spent practically every spare minute with you hoping that something romantic would happen, and nothing ever did,' she admits, shaking her head with frustration. 'I couldn't wait forever. I know it sounds pathetic now but I was falling so far behind all of my girlfriends. I needed to gain some practical experience with the opposite sex, just so I didn't become a social outcast. I didn't even have my first snog until I was seventeen!'

'If it helps, the event haunted me for a long time. I tortured myself for years afterwards, trying to work out how I could have handled things differently.'

'I remember exactly what you said to me that night,' admits Annie, her eyes rising to meet mine. In a completely natural reaction, I reach back across the table and hold onto her hand once more. She doesn't try to prevent me. Indeed, her fingers squeeze back tightly, sending a current of electricity coursing through my veins.

'This isn't our time,' we both recount, at almost exactly the same moment.

'Yeah,' she confirms.

'And then you disappeared off the face of the earth, and I didn't think it ever would be.'

'I'm here now, Annie,' I say with meaning. 'And I have no intention of going anywhere.'

'I'm glad to hear it,' she admits, a smile starting to spread across her features, which is instantly mirrored by my own.

'I know you see my desire whenever we look at each other,' I dare to state, watching her smile fade as her lips begin to quiver. 'Each brush of our fingertips. You must feel it? I certainly do. But now, you need to hear it.'

'Hear what?' she queries, in little more than a croak.

'I want you,' I admit boldly. 'Every time I see you. Every time I think of you. Every time I'm near you. Please never doubt that whenever we're together, I'm continuously having to stop myself from taking you into my arms and kissing you.'

For the longest few seconds of my life, I watch Annie's body language carefully, desperately trying to pick up some positive feedback following my wild declaration. Relief makes my heart beat loud and strong in my chest cavity, when she eventually shoots me a wicked smile and rises to her feet.

'In that case, I think it's probably time to leave, don't you?'

Hell yes!

Throwing a handful of notes on the table, I send her the briefest wink. Within seconds, we've been reunited with our coats and are making our way across the dark car park, hand in hand. Earlier, I abandoned my car in the far corner of the unlit area. It was done out of necessity rather than design; all of the other spaces were taken when we arrived, although there are plenty free now. But now, my earlier actions appear rather fortuitous.

Increasingly surrounded by darkness, we reach my car. I encourage Annie against the bodywork and playfully lean towards her.

'In my younger years, I always dreamed of being close to you,' I admit, feeling a thrill from the knowledge that our mouths are just inches apart, our breath combining. Of course, my admission is true.

But now, with a bit of life experience behind me, I know that the closeness I want to achieve with Annie isn't just a physical one. It's an emotional connection too, and we already have that in spades.

'How close?' she asks breathily, the ghost of a smile flitting across her face. 'Even closer than this?'

'Yes,' I grunt, further reducing the distance between us. 'As close as it's physically possible to be.'

'Oh God,' I hear her moan softly.

'If you don't stop me, I *am* going to kiss you,' I admit, aware of her breath ghosting across my face. 'Last chance,' I offer, as my fingers move into her hair, sensually cupping the back of her head. But Annie doesn't object. On the contrary, her panting breaths only seem to speed up. Reading her behaviour as a distinct green light, I close the distance between us, using my body to trap her more securely against the car. As our lips brush together for the first time, I hear both of us groan deeply as her mouth opens up to me.

Fuck. If I die now, I die the happiest of men.

CHAPTER 6

ANNIE

Is this seriously happening? I'm actually kissing Jack Harrison? I'm struggling to believe this isn't a dream, except I can feel the hard, angular shape of his car pressing against my shoulder and his warm mouth moving against mine, so I'm guessing this is actually real. I would pinch myself, just to be sure, but my hands are otherwise engaged. Currently busy exploring his incredible back and shoulders, I'm seriously grateful that Jack's solid physique is pinning me against the car, which is taking the bulk of my weight. With knees immobile and weak, thighs like jelly and my abdomen pulsing heavily, I couldn't be trusted to stand upright by my own volition, even if my life depended upon it. And yet despite that, I feel expectant and alert, ready for whatever wickedness Jack might deign to suggest next.

For the longest time, we just kiss for the sake of kissing. And what a kiss! It feels as though I'm living out every one of my adolescent fantasies, but this is no fantasy. This guy is one hundred percent real. Empathetic yet confident, natural yet intuitive, Jack is doing every-thing right while proving himself to be as sexy as hell. His tongue is a thing of wonder, and when it slides against my own, I can feel my pussy clenching hard. The sensation makes me desperate to enjoy more of his talents on an altogether more intimate part of my body.

This encounter represents all of my fantasies rolled into one delightful, highly delectable package. But in a strange way, I'm almost grateful that nothing happened when we were kids. No way would our coupling have *ever* been this good back then, for he couldn't see it; the desire silently pouring from me. The need to be held, admired, craved and accepted. But I'm pretty sure he gets it now.

Unwillingly, we eventually draw away from each other, largely as an opportunity to drag precious and much needed oxygen into our lungs.

'This isn't fair!' I complain in mock despair, stroking my hands through his hair as we continue to embrace intimately. It's as though neither of us can dare to let go of the treasure we have just discovered in each other. 'How can you possibly be even hotter than I thought you were, when I fancied you as a kid?'

My outburst immediately causes Jack to chuckle, his eyes briefly dropping down modestly, when confronted by my admission. I don't doubt he's thrilled though.

'You took the words right out of my mouth,' he mumbles, running a thumb tenderly down my cheek. 'Because literally nothing in this world compares to the way I feel when I kiss you. No person, no event, no memory, nothing. In the course of the past ten minutes, kissing you has become my all-time favourite hobby.'

I laugh from lighthearted happiness and also because I feel exactly the same way.

I tilt my mouth towards his once again and we revel in each other's kiss. But this time, it is even slower and more seductive than before. I can feel the arousal starting to seep through my panties, as my pussy swells and my nipples harden. I want Jack so badly. And I want him now. Every caress of his hand against my skin now generates a corresponding groan in the back of my throat. There is no hiding my desire, nor his by the feel of it. He's as hard as concrete.

I break our kiss, panting fast.

'I want you,' I admit. I'm demonstrating unusually wanton behaviour and I literally don't care. We've waited so long for this moment, I'm incapable of holding back for another second.

'I want you too, and I'm more than aware you want me,' he teases.

'How do you know?' I demand, not bothering to counter that I know he wants me too. After all, what would be the point? The evidence has been enthusiastically digging into my thigh for quite some time.

'A number of reasons, really,' he admits, his tone low and intimate. 'You were flushed over dinner, even though the restaurant was relatively cool. Your tone, your breathing, the way we couldn't keep our eyes off each other. They were all clues. And now that I'm pressed up close against you, I can smell your arousal.'

Jack unexpectedly lets out a low, deep growl which speaks to me on a purely primal level, making every cell of my body vibrate in response.

'Oh God,' I breathe, needing whatever the hell Jack is offering.

'And it's turning me on something chronic,' he admits. 'Honestly, all I can think about right now is tasting you.'

I swallow hard, gazing up into his eyes imploringly.

'But we aren't doing this here,' he continues, correctly reading my hesitation. 'Would you like to go somewhere more private?'

'Yes,' I manage to voice. 'I would like that very much.'

Having pinned me so successfully to the car for such a long time, Jack slowly peels his large, masculine physique away, opens the passenger door and assists me inside. Within seconds of driving away, he scoops my hand into his and lays it upon his muscular thigh, to enable us to remain in close contact. Aware that my fingers are now inches away from his incredibly hard cock, I feel the tips of them start to tingle. I don't want to cause an accident, but at the same time, the temptation is ultimately likely to become too much. But, in the worst possible way, that temptation is removed when my mobile phone starts to ring.

Glancing down at the screen lit up in the surrounding darkness, I can see the caller is Lee. Given Toby is currently staying the night at my ex's house, I simply have to answer, just in case something has happened to my son. It's a no brainer.

'I'm sorry but I do have to take this,' I mutter, before retracting my hand away from Jack while trying to quell my naturally anxious maternal instinct. 'Hello?'

'I think something's wrong with Toby.' There is no attempt to be civil or to prepare me for what would obviously be a huge shock. Lee just comes straight out with it, causing my blood pressure to leap from normal to critical in the space of a single second.

'Oh my God! What's happened?'

I sense Jack moving beside me, trying to tune into the call, but I make no attempt to communicate with him. All that matters right now is my son.

'I'm not sure, but I think you should come to my house straight away.'

'I'm on my way,' I confirm, hanging up.

'What's wrong?' Jack asks instantly, his voice full of genuine concern.

'Not sure, but I need to get over to Lee's house. Can you drop me home, please?'

'I'll do one better than that,' offers Jack. 'I'll take you straight there if you can give me directions?'

Fortunately, Lee's house isn't far away and we're there within ten minutes. Sensibly, Jack offers to wait in the car, while I dash towards the front door. I guess Lee must have been watching out for me because I'm granted entry with almost indecent haste.

'Where is he?' I demand, surprised to see Toby standing sheepishly behind his father, the instant I cross the threshold. Dashing across to him, I fall to my knees and pull him into my arms.

'Are you okay, Darling?' I ask gently. 'What's happened?'

'I'm fine, Mum,' replies Toby, looking rather bemused. 'I'm not sure why Dad called you. All I did was mention that you were having dinner with Mr Harrison.'

My eyes flash darkly towards Lee and he fails to hide his guilty expression. Toby might not be able to account for the details, but I can see *exactly* what's happened. Having discovered that I was enjoying my first date since we broke up over a year ago, Lee decided he wanted to put a stop to it.

'Well, you'd better get your bits together and I'll take you home. Unless you want to stay here with Daddy?' I see Toby shake his head almost imperceptibly, before dashing upstairs to gather his possessions.

'Now hang on!' Lee begins to argue. 'You can't just come in here and...'

But I'm not in the mood for his particular brand of bullshit this evening. I was having a fantastic time with Jack, but thanks to Lee's selfish jealousy, he broke our buoyant, happy moods, as well as our perfect evening.

'If you honestly believe Toby is ill enough that you need to call me, then I'm taking our son home with me to look after him,' I explain.

'No...no...I didn't mean...'

'Tough,' I snap, trying to keep my voice quiet, so Toby doesn't have to hear his parents bickering...again. 'You can't have it both ways, Lee. Either you're looking after him, or you're not. If I'm ultimately responsible for Tobes, then that's fine. I will be. I want to be. But don't you *dare* use him to get to me again. You don't get to fuck around with my life anymore.'

Sensibly, Lee chooses not to respond, so we stand there staring at each other for a few seconds, listening to our son's footsteps padding around on the floor above. It's becoming patently clear to me that this situation with Lee isn't working. For years now, I've known he's a hugely toxic influence in my life, and to some extent in Toby's too, which is the reason I ultimately left him. But he's gone too far tonight. It's ironic really, that he should have an issue about me starting to date again after we're divorced, when he thought it was acceptable to screw around within wedlock.

I observe his narrow, somewhat spiteful eyes, balding head and grimace, and compare him rather unfavourably to the man waiting for us in the car outside. What the hell was I thinking when I married Lee? The two men are like chalk and cheese; incomparable. Although, of course, Jack hadn't been in my life back then. I'd believed him to be lost to me, like an imaginary friend from my childhood. A little too good to be true. But he's back with a vengeance now. Boy is he back!

A small smile starts to grace my lips at the memory of our exquisite kiss, before I shut it down. The last thing I need is Lee getting the wrong impression that I'm smiling at him.

Lee. Instantly, the shutters fall down on my good mood. I simply have to determine a different way to interact with my ex-husband. For the sake of my son, we obviously need to maintain contact, but not like this. And then inspiration strikes me.

'I'm getting a new phone number tomorrow,' I state, the idea still not fully formed by the time I share it. 'Our direct communication will now happen by email only.'

Getting a new number is a nuisance, but it's the only way I can see to navigate around the problem. There are relatively few people in my world to inform of this change, so other than admin stuff like online banking, switching phone numbers isn't as much of a nightmare as it might be for some people. And well worth it for my peace of mind in the future. We might share a son together, but I can't allow Lee to continue to negatively impact my life now we're divorced. He did quite enough damage while we were married. Enough is enough.

'What if there's an emergency?' he objects, the anger I know so well starting to seep into his tone.

'My mother will be the emergency contact. If there really is an emergency, she will get hold of me.'

This is actually a masterstroke. Lee has always been somewhat in awe of my mum who is as straight talking as they come. There is no way he'd try to pull a stunt like he has tonight, with her. And although I haven't asked mum yet, I instinctively know she'll be happy with the arrangement. I can almost hear her response now, imploring me, as always, to get on with my life and find my own happiness. So many times over the years, I've explained that I am trying. Tonight, with Jack, might I be on the first step to succeeding? Another smile threatens to cross my features. My mum always *adored* Jack during our younger years; God, if we get together, she'll be unbearable!

'You're not seriously thinking of dating our son's teacher are you?'

Lee's voice snaps me out of my happy place, straight back into reality with a crash. I observe him coolly, wondering what the hell I was ever thinking when I decided he was the right man for me. Life is short and in recent years, I haven't been living it. At least, not to the best of my abilities. I've been allowing mundane upset and particularly Lee's unacceptable attitude to encroach on my wellbeing, but that just isn't good enough anymore. Both for Toby's sake, but also my own. I've known for some time that things had to change in my life. I have a sneaking suspicion that Jack might well become the catalyst for that long-awaited change.

'What I am, or am not planning to do, is no longer any concern of yours. The only subject you and I ever need to discuss is the wellbeing and welfare of our son. Beyond that, all conversation stops. And the sooner you get that into your head, the better for all of us, including Toby.' Fortunately, this outburst is little more than a hiss by the time I finish, ensuring a returning Tobes doesn't overhear his parents at war.

'Come on, Sweetheart,' I say gently, as his soft brown eyes meet mine on the stairs, bag in his hand. 'Say goodbye to Daddy and then we'll get straight home. It's *way* past your bedtime.'

CHAPTER 7

JACK

Annie's home is charming. That's the only word I can think of to describe it. Warm, friendly, tidy and clean, it also manages to give the impression of being lived-in and welcoming. While Annie's been upstairs settling Toby into bed, I've made myself useful in the kitchen, putting on the kettle and locating the necessary items to make a coffee. Noting she has cream in her fridge and Irish whiskey in a glass-fronted dresser, I take the management decision to upgrade our beverages accordingly. After the squabble she's had with Lee, I'm guessing she'll appreciate it.

Our car journey home was somewhat stilted. Toby and I shared a conversation to fill the silence, but I'm sure he realised something was wrong. Kids aren't stupid; they always know. I'd offered to drop them both off and leave, but Annie was insistent that I join them. To be honest, I think she needs a friendly face to talk to, rather than sitting up alone and brooding tonight. And I'm more than happy to provide a shoulder to cry on. After all, as far as I'm concerned, first and foremost, I am her friend. By the time I hear Annie's soft steps making their way down the stairs, two Irish coffees are sitting on the kitchen work surface.

'Your ex is an arse,' I observe, smiling across at her. Collecting the two mugs, I follow her through to the lounge and we collapse down on the sofa at opposite ends.

'I know,' she sighs. 'He didn't used to be.'

She accepts the beverage I've made her and gratefully inhales the steam. I smile at her reaction when she realises the coffee is an alcoholic one.

'Unfortunately for me, he's also Toby's father which means for at least the next eight years, I need to maintain a civil line of open communication with him.'

'I understand completely,' I reply. In any relationship which includes children, they have to come first. No question. 'Not much fun for you though.'

'Fun?' she asks, accompanied by an empty laugh. 'Life isn't about fun, is it? It's about responsibility.'

'It can be about fun too, Annie,' I explain gently. I watch her take a sip of the warming drink, a little groan of pleasure audible as the alcohol hits the back of her throat. 'Toby is a beautifully brought up, well-rounded little boy. I work with him every day and I can see the positive influence you've had on his character, attitude and morals. You've done an amazing job.'

'Thank you,' she whispers, tears daring to prickle her eyes.

'You need to cut yourself a break.'

'You sound just like my mum!' she admits, with a broken laugh, before taking another restorative sip.

'Maybe you need to take note of the people who have your best interests at heart?' I suggest. 'Because they're right.'

'I don't think I know how to be anything but this.' Her sigh is long and deep and I sense also a little despairing. Why is it that the person we are often the least sympathetic to is ourselves?

'Yeah, it's tough, isn't it?' The note of sympathy in my tone is unmistakable. Leaning towards the coffee table, I reach for a small yellow rose which is nestling in a bouquet there. I recognise the bloom as one of the climbing flowers arching over Annie's front door. She must have picked these for herself, in order to brighten up the room. Instantly, I have an urge to purchase her a huge bunch of flowers, to declare how I feel. Followed by another bunch, for every day that follows.

'But sometimes, you just have to stop and smell the roses.' I pass the delicate flower across to her. Accepting it, she raises it to her nose and inhales deeply, closing her eyes with pleasure.

'Life is short. Life is precious. But life is good.'

'I haven't really lived for so long,' she explains sadly, shaking her head. 'Tonight with you...'

'Yes?' I encourage, wanting to hear more.

'Well...it was the first time I've felt alive in...oh...I don't know how many years.'

I place my empty mug back down on the table. The alcohol is starting to take effect and I feel undaunted and bold.

'I can show you happiness if you want.'

'What do you mean?'

'Oh, come on Annie!' I cajole, shifting my hips slightly to face her more easily. 'You know how I feel about you. You must have always known.' As she gazes towards me in open-mouthed astonishment, I take advantage of the stunned silence to press on. 'I want to see you smile again. In fact, I'll do just about anything I can to make that happen.'

'I feel like I'm a mess right now.'

'You're more together than you know,' I tell her honestly, reaching across to take her hand. 'But I'm not going to rush you. I'll wait for as long as it takes.' And that is God's honest truth.

'What did I ever do, to deserve you as my friend?' she sighs, bending down to lean her forehead against the back of my hand. I can sense her pain and confusion.

'Hey! What we have goes both ways you know. Now, stop feeling sorry for yourself,' I order in my strictest, school teacher voice. It seems to do the trick. Sitting up straighter, she glances across at me and our eyes lock.

'You're quite right. My priority has always been, and will always be Toby, but I'd like to be happy too. Is that a selfish thing to admit?'

'Of course not,' I reply soothingly, my respect for Annie growing by the second. The exalted position which Toby holds in her life is clear, and that's exactly how it should be. I mean, why bring children into the world if you can't love, protect and care for them to the very best of your ability? But Annie is right; she's important too. I start to stroke the back of her hand with my thumb. It's only supposed to be a supportive gesture, but going by the way Annie's face starts to flush, I'm guessing that isn't the way she's reading the situation.

'Initially, in my marriage, I had been happy,' she admits, her voice breaking slightly as my thumb slides along to the delicate skin of her wrist. 'But when Lee and I truly started falling apart, and he didn't even try to hide the fact he was screwing around, life got tough. Indeed, on some of those days, Toby was the only bright light on an otherwise very dark existence. And now my life is finally starting to look good again, Lee's trying to fuck things up at every given opportunity. I'm sorry! I'm sure this is way too much of a messy situation for you to get involved in.' Her apology is concluded by a frustrated huff that makes me smile gently. She really has no idea, does she?

'Annie, I learnt from my mistake twenty years ago. You have to fight for what you want...for the person you want to be with,' I correct, continuing to speak gently. 'But fighting takes many forms. Sometimes it's action and other times it's patience. And I have patience.'

Annie's eyes are turning slightly glassy now and I have an urge to scoop her up into my arms and never let her go. She opens her mouth to respond, but clearly can't find the words, so I continue.

'So, if you want me to step back until the situation with your ex is resolved, or until Toby is older, I will do that. I *can* do that. Just so long as I know that at the end of it, you and I have a shot together.' Although this statement is true, I silently acknowledge it will be agony to follow through with. My strength of desire has not faded with age. In fact, you could argue that it's grown ever stronger, and continues to do so on an hourly basis.

'But I don't want to wait,' she protests.

Thank God.

'Me neither. I'm struggling to resist you. I don't want to resist you...' I admit, my grip around her wrist growing stronger. 'It's killing me right now, not to take you into my arms and kiss you.'

'Then do it. Please,' she requests breathily. 'Please.'

'But if I start, how can I ever bear to stop,' I groan, the deep sound reverberating up my throat full of pained longing. We both know Toby's upstairs asleep and no way can I allow our first time to be in his presence. That wouldn't be fair on any of us.

'We will,' mutters Annie, sliding her hand around mine and pulling me towards her. 'Please, Jack. Please.'

'Oh God.' My groan sounds as though the last defences have been ripped from my body which, I suppose in a way, they have. In one smooth movement, I travel across the short distance which separates us. Encouraging Annie into a horizontal position, I cradle her jaw gently in my hand and encourage our lips closer. I'm holding my weight above her as best I can, but the low, satisfied groan I hear escaping from Annie as I trap her beneath me, confirms I don't need to worry. She wants this equally as much as I do. And there's no hiding just how much I desire her; I am achingly hard.

Just before our lips brush together, I become conscious of her warm breath dancing across my face. The situation is beyond thrilling. I feel seriously lightheaded, although I have to acknowledge that's probably because all the blood is being diverted away from my brain, towards a more demanding part of my anatomy. And then our mouths combine into something more heavenly than anything imaginable, and I am lost. I've travelled the world, always searching for that missing something, only to discover it within the arms of my childhood friend. At last, after years in the wilderness, I am home.

CHAPTER 8

ANNIE

Powerless to resist and certainly not wanting to, I'm pinned to the sofa, quite literally revelling in the feel of Jack's magnificent body. The majority of his weight is being held up by those powerful arms I've previously admired, allowing my own hands to explore. If my mouth wasn't busy kissing him, there would be a huge grin plastered across my face, particularly at the low groan he emits, every time I squeeze his scrumptious ass.

As things heat up further, I'm becoming aware of every touch point our writhing bodies share; our mouths, chins, my breasts pressing against his broad chest, our hips and thighs. Not to mention the swollen protrusion which is growing increasingly hard between us, courtesy of the incredible man lying above me. I never really doubted him but now I have physical proof; Jack yearns for me equally as much as I do for him, and that knowledge is completely thrilling.

There is certainly no shortage of evidence that we want to fuck each other, hard and often. But equally, I'm not being made to feel that there's an urgent rush to do so. It's a refreshing and life-affirming realisation to know that for both of us, exploring each other in this way is quite enough for now. More than enough; it's fucking fantastic.

The biggest thrill I can ever remember. Jack tastes so smooth and masculine, yet sweet. I honestly don't think I've ever desired another human being so much in my entire life, and I know I won't feel this way again. Jack is the pinnacle of my sexual desire; my every wish come true.

We revel in the unfamiliarity of each other's mouths, overwhelmed by the shapes and sensations we can create by combining our tongues and lips. The desire and excitement is literally exploding joyously from me. Perhaps it helps that I haven't known real intimacy for the longest time, or that Jack is my childhood sweetheart. Or maybe our bodies are just meant to be forevermore entwined. Certainly, as a younger woman, kissing had never been this daring, fun or exciting. Being here like this with Jack is something new. Something I could certainly get used to enjoying in my life, ideally on a daily basis.

Over time, with increasing confidence, our passion slowly expands from a gently flickering flame into an all-round inferno. We are acting like two people who have never enjoyed intimacy before, suddenly needing to experience everything in a heady, addictive rush. Not just hungry for each other now, we are apparently famished, as we each feed off the other's infinite desires. Hands, mouths, teeth, tongues; all are used in a frantic bid to become as close as two humans can possibly be. So much for thinking just kissing is enough. Right now, only one question dominates my thoughts; do we make love here on the sofa, or in my bedroom?

I have no idea how long we kiss for but with reluctance, Jack eventually draws back. I'm instantly conscious of my face being slightly sore from his stubble grinding continuously against it, but I care not. It's the sweetest discomfort I've ever known. Panting gently, we stare at each other hungrily, our eyes ablaze with passion. I don't doubt what he wants; right now, I am utterly confident that his dirty, wicked desires are entirely aligned with my own.

'I need to take you upstairs to bed,' I say, my frantic craving making me bold and brave.

'Oh fuck,' he groans, as though the thought causes him actual physical pain. The pain of having to resist. 'You've got no idea how much I want that too. But not here. Not now. It isn't fair on any of us.' Instinctively, I realise Jack's use of the word *us* includes Toby and my ardour dampens slightly.

I huff with annoyance, but I know he's doing the right thing, no matter how frustrating it might be. After all, we had previously come to a mutual agreement that nothing was going to happen tonight, although I don't doubt that we both need a damn sight more.

'Okay,' I agree unwillingly. 'But can you at least stay over? I want to hold you all night.'

This suggestion is unexpectedly met by Jack's mirthless laughter.

'You're joking, right?'

'No,' I reply, shaking my head in confusion.

'Yeah, that's not gonna happen.'

'Why?'

'Annie, if you seriously think I can lay beside you all night and not touch you...not kiss you,' he explains, stroking a hand softly down my face, which sets off all kinds of chemical reactions in my body. '...and not make you come apart in my arms, then you have no idea how I feel about you.'

He's got a fair point. After all, that is exactly the same way I feel about him, if I'm being honest.

'So, tell me how you feel,' I challenge, flashing him a cheeky grin. As always, Jack doesn't disappoint.

'I want to make you scream for me,' he admits, in a rare moment of total honesty. Just hearing those words sends darts of elation exploding across my skin, making my clit throb harder than ever. 'I need to see you disintegrate beneath me with a pleasure that only I can bring you.'

FUCK.

I have no response. Panting is literally the only way I can communicate right now as I subconsciously start to grind my pelvis against Jack's hard body. My fingernails dig into his shoulders in an attempt to anchor myself to something dependably secure, while my entire reality sways and lurches out of control. Rightly assuming his dirty admissions are working very effectively, Jack makes no attempt to stem his suggestive words.

'I want to sink myself incredibly deep inside of you and stay there forever and a day,' he grunts. Pushing his hips against my own, he electrifies the sensations my movements earn, making me gasp with delight. But he's not done turning me on with his words yet.

'I want to feel you squeezing me, milking me, begging me for more as I move inside you. And every single one of your reactions will only make me fuck you harder.'

Geez. The guy is dynamite.

'Fuck,' I groan. He's my drug; the one thing I can't live without and pretty much the most addictive person on the planet. I've gone without my fix for the past two decades and I'm sure as hell not willing to go without any longer. With an impassioned moan, I drag his mouth back to mine and we kiss as though our lives depend on it. This time, we display even less control and things start to get out of hand. Eventually, Jack breaks our kiss, only to slide his mouth down the side of my neck towards one of my throbbing nipples. I whimper shamelessly, needing this. Wanting more. Desiring exactly what he'd threatened earlier. I'm so swollen and wet for him. Literally, the only thing that has a chance of stemming the overwhelming ache inside, is to feel him ploughing into me, stretching me and fucking me hard.

'I really should go,' he moans, stopping just inches from his anticipated target.

'No, please,' I beg, using my hands to try and guide him into position. But Jack sends me a regretful smile and remains where he is. His breath is bouncing across the thin blouse covering my chest. I can see his pupils contracting and dilating, every unique eyelash. We are *so* close and he is making no visible attempt to move away.

'You know I can't,' he says gently. 'But equally, I can't walk away from here tonight without having firm plans to see you again. Properly. Will you come away with me?'

'What do you mean?' I gasp, tightening my grip on his shoulders.

'Come away for a night with me, when you don't have Toby,' he clarifies.

'You mean like a dirty weekend?' I can't help but smirk. The whole idea sounds so delightfully devilish.

'Yeah...but it'll be a filthy one,' he confirms. Just the way he says it – softly, temptingly – practically has me dragging him up to my bedroom then and there, and damn the consequences. And the way his mischievously dancing eyes are watching me sends an instant explosion of excitement coursing through my veins. He means that. Boy, does he mean that. I can see the lust and desire bubbling beneath the surface, almost as clearly as I can see his face. And let me tell you, it's a heady feeling to know that somebody wants me this much. Has possibly always wanted me this much. And the feeling is a mutual one. There hasn't been a day in the last twenty years that Jack hasn't existed in my universe. Maybe not consciously so, every single day, but he's certainly been there. And now what? We get to play out our teenage crush for real, as adults? How sweet is this going to be? The idea is too heady to even contemplate.

'I need to know when you're free,' he presses. 'When can we get away?'

'Well, hardly ever,' I huff. When Toby's at school, so will Jack be. And when Jack's not working, I'll largely be responsible for Toby. Finding time together in a secret capacity is always going to present a challenge.

'Bummer,' grins Jack, reverting to one of our childhood phrases.

'But Toby is staying with his grandparents next weekend,' I explain, grabbing at that knowledge like a lifeline.

'Might I take you away for the weekend, then?' he asks, looking a little anxious. My response obviously means a great deal to him. 'Unless you're otherwise engaged?'

'I...' Involuntarily, I stutter my response. Suddenly, the enormity of what he's suggesting has hit me. Jack Harrison wants to take me away on a weekend together, for the sole purpose of us enjoying each other's bodies.

'Please...I'm dying here. I need you,' he implores.

'Okay,' I whisper. But my voice fails on the first attempt, so I try again. 'Yes, thank you.' In my stunned state, my reply is still barely audible, but the wide grin which spreads across his face confirms Jack has heard me all the same. We kiss again, but this time the hot passion has gone. Instead, our movements are slow, tender and incredibly loving. Tears dare to prickle my eyelids as I'm forced to appreciate that Jack is experiencing the same depth of feeling as I am.

'I really should go,' he mutters, finally breaking away. I'm pleased to see his eyes are as glassy as mine. It is comforting to know that I'm not alone in this maelstrom of emotions.

'We've wasted so much time,' I observe, trying not to sob.

'But we've found each other again now,' he counters quickly. 'And that's all that matters. This is only the beginning. There is no reason to be sad here, Annie. Only absurdly happy.'

'I really don't want you to leave.'

'And I *really* don't want to go,' he acknowledges. 'But you know this is the right thing to do. It isn't fair on Toby to have his Geography teacher sharing cornflakes and toast over the breakfast table tomorrow morning, without warning or explanation.'

I nod, a wave of heat passing through my chest in acknowledgement for the way I feel about Jack. My adoration for the man only grows stronger, knowing that he's prioritising the requirements of my precious son over his own substantial needs. Standing, we rearrange our clothing as best we can, before making our way towards the front door. There, Jack takes me into his arms and holds me close. Our proximity fills me with a strength that makes me believe I can take on just about anything in the world.

'I'll see you very soon,' he murmurs into my ear, before dropping a final kiss on my forehead and opening the door.

Unwillingly, I watch him walk up the garden path, before he pauses and once more turns to face me.

'Oh, and Annie?' he adds, gazing back at me with adoration.

'Yeah?' I croak.

'*This* is our time.'

CHAPTER 9

ANNIE

'Oh, my darling!' My mother embraces me so tightly that it almost makes me cry. She's always hugged me like she means it but right now, I have no doubt of the depth of her affection. 'I'm so pleased you've decided to look after yourself for a change. Going away will be just the tonic you need, to stop you thinking about the whole messy Lee situation.' Mum returns to her seat and shakes her head slightly, as though trying to erase the thought of my ex-husband. If only it were that easy.

'Thanks Mum.'

'So, who are you going with? Janice? Sarah? Emily?' she enquires, moving us ever closer to the part of the conversation I've been dreading. How exactly do you inform a parent that you're going away on a dirty weekend? Biting the bullet; that's how.

'Well, er, actually. It's with a guy.'

'Oh!' I'm immediately surprised by her reaction. Far from looking shocked, she looks positively jubilant. 'A weekend away with a man? And do I know him?'

It's a fair enough question, given I'd previously informed her I was going away with an old school friend.

'It's Jack,' I admit.

'Oh my goodness! Really?' My mother doesn't say anything more, but I can see from her expression that she's beyond thrilled. In fact, she looks almost smug.

'Yeah, really. It turns out he's one of Toby's teachers. We met up a little while ago and I want to take it further.'

'I always knew,' she mumbles.

'What did you always know?' I demand, staring at her until she responds.

'That the two of you would eventually end up together.'

'Hey! Hold on! That's jumping the gun a little bit, even for you!' I'm not surprised by her reaction, but I have to object. She's always adored Jack. Indeed, they used to have quite a mutual appreciation society going on, spending many happy hours sitting around the kitchen table, drinking cups of tea, eating cookies and sharing the local gossip.

'Sorry, Darling. I hope you have a wonderful, wonderful time together. I don't expect he's changed much, has he?' she muses. 'At least I hope he hasn't. Jack always was the nicest boy.'

'Thanks Mum,' I grin, unable to hide my delight. 'He was. And he's grown into an even nicer man.'

I'M grateful we're travelling in Jack's car for our weekend away because I'm *way* too wired to drive safely. My body is simply brimming with adrenaline, lust and fire. Gazing at the countryside flashing past outside the window I hide a smirk, wondering if Jack has any idea what he's let himself in for. From earlier conversations, he seems to be planning a romantic walk along the beach when we arrive, followed by dinner together. I'm not going to burst his bubble quite yet, but I have no intention of following that schedule. We've waited too long. The instant we step into our hotel room to drop off our luggage, the guy is in serious trouble.

I am waxed, shaved and plucked to within an inch of my life. I've even been to the hairdresser, although with any luck, my hair will be so messed up by this evening that you'll never be able to tell.

Suddenly, with a smirk, I try to call a halt to such seriously slutty thoughts which aren't really like me. But the excitement is bursting out; I don't want to hide my desires anymore and I don't actually know if I can. I want to make love to Jack. I've always wanted him. And today, it is going to happen at last.

The boutique hotel doesn't disappoint. A beautiful Tudor-style building, it is nestled in the hills above a tranquil English fishing community. From our slightly elevated location, I can see the pretty village adorned in sun, bordered by a stretch of golden sandy beach which curves around into a small bay. The gentle clinking of the fishing boats in a distant harbour, as metal rigging taps against masts, helps to round off the perfect scene. And it is perfect, but not as much as the guy I'm with, and it's him that deserves my full attention right now. Having checked in and taken ownership of the key, the butterflies positively explode in my tummy when the door of our room closes behind us and Jack places the luggage on the rack.

'So, I thought maybe we could...' he starts to explain.

But that's as far as I let him get. Winding my arms around his neck, I press my lips against his, simultaneously guiding us towards the bed. Jack responds with a low, satisfied groan, leaving no question that this is also the activity he would much prefer to engage in. Our kiss is hungry, frenzied and at a different tempo than every kiss we've ever shared before. Because this time, we both understand that nothing is holding us back. No ex-husbands, no school, no Toby. No barriers. This time, Jack and myself are truly alone together, all our emotions laid bare.

'You're my dream come true,' he mutters, as we begin to work the clothing from each other's bodies. I can only groan in response, having temporarily lost the ability to speak. But given I'm unwrapping Jack for the very first time, perhaps my reaction is forgivable. Edging his shirt away, I uncover his gorgeous shoulders and upper arms which are satisfyingly muscled, but not overly so. Light hairs scattered across his chest, narrow down to a line that disappears beneath the waistband of his jeans, presumably onto even tastier treats. I feel as though that line of hair is acting like a signpost, attempting to lead me astray and explore further. Like I need that kind of encouragement?

'Oh fuck. You're so beautiful,' he admits breathlessly. Kissing me intermittently, he unclasps my bra, stroking the straps from my arms to reveal my throbbing nipples. This is just too much. I can feel the heat between my legs multiplying at an exponential rate, as my panties become soaked with arousal for the only man who has ever really done it for me. And then without giving any notice whatsoever, his mouth deviates away from mine and heads south.

Our joint low groan is the very epitome of ecstasy. I'm mindful of Jack kissing gently around my breasts as I tremble beneath his focused attention. When he finally teases one hardened nipple between his lips and sucks tenderly, I react with eagerness. Gasping, my hands instantly tighten around his shoulders. Meanwhile, my hips start to rock, moulding my body against his and pushing my wanton flesh further into his mouth. With a growl, Jack willingly accepts the challenge, using a spare hand to increase the pressure and maximising my thrill. Having satisfied one throbbing breast, he slides across to the other, kissing and muttering as he goes. I just manage to make out his words.

'God. You taste fucking amazing, Annie. Sweeter than I'd even imagined.'

Dizzy and aroused, I have to keep reminding myself that although I am living my fantasy right now, this is also actually happening. Every second, every minute in this incredible man's company is real. The thrill is almost too much to contemplate, so I purposefully push the thought away to concentrate on other things. Besides, I don't have any space for logical thought right now. I'm operating on adrenaline and pure lust alone.

During the entire time my nipples are being skilfully adored by Jack's remarkable mouth, I find myself in a disbelieving state of suspense, unable to resist the pleasure being bestowed upon me. Only when he releases me am I able to think again. Automatically, as our hungry mouths rejoin and our lips mesh back together, my hands quite naturally sink lower. Having wrestled with the fastenings of

Jack's button-fly jeans, one by one I pop them open, highly aware of a swollen mass which lies beneath the soft material. I feel so goddam aroused that I'm grateful to be horizontal, else I might faint.

I waste no time in discarding his trousers and with some joint effort, within what feels like seconds, we are both naked. The first time our bodies entwine, warm skin grazing against warm skin, I gasp. This is like nothing I've ever known before. We fit together with utter perfection, almost as though our union is meant to be. I can feel my breasts squashing against his warm chest and our hips interlocking. My legs crawl easily up Jack's thighs, swiftly trapping him into a location that I have no desire for him to ever leave. Our kiss is ravenous now; teeth, tongues, lips, all working in harmony with each other, in order to maximise the euphoria of the moment. With a cry of despair, I know I can stand the suspense no longer. I have to increase our bond further. I need to taste him.

Unwillingly dragging my mouth away from Jack's, I push him back onto the mattress and crawl down his magnificent body, kissing every available part of him as I go; his chiselled jaw, smooth neck, incredible shoulders, broad chest, and what I discover are well-defined abs. There is no denying that the guy works out. When I reach his tummy, Jack's breathing alters significantly. Audibly becoming faster and more shallow, it is now interlaced with the occasional groan which sets my soul on fire. Yes, this is what I need. I know this man so well but there is one emotion I have never witnessed in him: ecstasy. The one facet of Jack Harrison's personality that I desire to know intimately. Over and over and over again.

For the first time, I dare to glance down at the thick protrusion my chest is pressed up against. I swallow hard at the sight, my internal muscles automatically clenching hard. He's thick and long. But then, that's hardly surprising, is it? That my perfect man has the perfect cock? I shake my head gently. This is a dream; it has to be. I would pinch myself but my hand is already in use, starting to wrap itself around the best gift ever. The one I wish to consume at my leisure.

'Oh God, Annie!' Jack's words are whispered weakly into the room, his hand gently caressing the back of my head. I hold myself over him, glancing up into his adoring eyes. It's a scenario I wish to commit to my long-term memory. The experience of pure intimacy between two fated lovers. Two people who were always destined to be together.

I smile gently at him but the sentiment is not returned. Jack doesn't seem capable of reacting at present, thanks to his wide eyes and openly panting mouth. I *love* that I can get him into this state and I adore wielding this level of control over him. Moving slightly closer, hovering above, I watch him react accordingly. Deciding that I've probably tormented him for long enough, my tongue slips out for just a second, to caress his smooth, throbbing head. Instantly Jack's eyes close, as though the powerful sensation requires him to shut down every other facet of his personality. I can't say I blame him; I don't doubt I'd be in exactly the same mental state of agony myself. Not that my empathy is going to cause me to take it easy. Quite the opposite, in fact. As though to prove a point, I work my mouth against him a little longer this time, encouraging the most delicious of groans from his mouth.

'Ohmigod,' I hear him stutter.

Precum has already started to leak from the slit and I lap it up greedily, consuming with enthusiasm. A deep growl echoes low down in my own throat, which almost exactly matches that escaping from Jack's. I want to partake in this enjoyment forever.

CHAPTER 10

JACK

So close.

I'm so *fucking* close to coming, it's unreal.

Annie has been torturously holding me on the edge for so long...too long. I'm throbbing hard, breathless and *so* big. Blood has rushed from my brain to an area my body deems is currently much more important, and I literally can't think of anything else but her. I keep trying to encourage Annie back up the bed so I can pleasure her in return but she continuously prevents me. And to be quite honest, I'm too weak to resist right now.

I have no doubt that what I'm experiencing is the very definition of heaven. Being with the woman I love and knowing that she desires me equally. Could anything in life be better than this? Of course, I know there's an answer to that: Yes. Mutual arousal would be even better. The realisation empowers me, providing the necessary willpower to react. Holding Annie by the shoulders I gently encourage her upwards, as I wriggle down the bed slightly. At last, the spell is broken, if only temporarily, and I am able to think clearly. Able to breathe again.

'I'm gonna pay you back for that,' I mutter into her ear, as I continue to push her up the bed. And I mean it. I hear her whimper in response to my dirty threat, and the seductive sound fills me with determination.

Travelling down her mouth-watering curves, nipping and nibbling as I go, Annie's heat and aroma grows stronger. I growl, unable to fight my animal instincts. I simply *have* to taste her. My lover is obviously much noisier than me, which is perfect. I intuitively know that hearing her cries of ecstasy will only drive me on to greater heights. Without delay, I push her thighs wide open and settle myself into the optimum position, my mouth already salivating for a taste.

'Oh God,' she whimpers, fingers sliding through my hair.

Say goodbye to your self-control, I don't utter, as my lips start to stroke tenderly across her wetness. Instantly, I feel Annie's entire body judder, her lungs already being forced to work hard as she drags in much-needed air. I'm mindful of her prominent clit, although I purposefully avoid touching it. The state she's in causes me to deduce that our previous activities must have seriously turned her on. It's a thrilling realisation.

Gradually, I sink my tongue deeper and deeper into her swollen folds. When I eventually start to push inside her, her pussy quivers, Annie's heavy breathing noticeably moving towards shrieks. She is so wet, so addictive, and *so* close. Visibly on the verge of losing control now, Annie isn't holding back. Her cries fill our room, her pussy clenching and pulsating around my tongue as she writhes against me, desperate for more. If I was feeling playful, I'd make her wait. I'd keep building up her desire, before denying, time and time again. And I will do that...soon. But this first time, I don't want to play games. After years of being with the wrong men, I need her to feel the abundant joy of being with the right one. If she can stand the intensity, that is.

Knowing I'll need to hold her firmly in place before I start, I quickly shift position. Linking one arm around her thigh to open her wide, I press down lightly, trapping her firmly in place. Then, as my lips move up to hover over her clit, I press two fingers gently against her sopping pussy.

'You ready for this?' I murmur, but the only response I receive is a satisfied grunt. I guess that will have to be good enough.

Without delay, I suckle her previously neglected clit between my lips, to be lovingly tended to by my responsive tongue. Immediately, Annie twists beneath me, but my arm has a good hold of her. Entirely trapped, she has no option but to absorb the inexhaustible supply of bliss that I intend to bestow upon her. Roaring with desire, it's obvious she's just about to explode, her first of many climaxes mere seconds away. So I take the opportunity to sink two thick fingers deep inside, revelling in the sensation of her muscles grasping me tightly as the orgasm takes hold

I work Annie hard that afternoon, never once stopping as I encourage her to ride the crest of an extended orgasm. Stabbing my fingers deep, I focus on her G-spot as her clit continues to be clamped within my mouth. Ultimately, I know I have to pause, but each time she erupts with ecstasy, the sound of her cries make it obvious that she still needs more. Having never been intimate with Annie before in this way, it's surprising that I can read her desires so accurately, but I know I can. Just the sounds she's making and the extreme reactions of her body, as she claws and grasps at my head for mercy, are good enough for me.

At long, long last, I retract. The woman I shuffle up the bed beside is a shadow of her former self; sweating, red-faced, panting heavily and trembling out of control, this is exactly how I want to see Annie, every time she comes to bed with me in the future.

'That...was....' She pauses as yet another aftershock traverses through her, ramping Annie's levels of physical pleasure sky high again, even though I'm no longer touching her. 'Fuck...ing...a...maz...ing,' she eventually manages to conclude.

'Good,' I smile, my happiness seeping out of every pore. 'Now, do you need to rest, or do you need my cock?' I offer, impishly. I honestly do understand if she needs to rest, given what I've just made her endure, but simply to lessen my own extreme levels of frustration, I hope to God she chooses the latter. I am achingly hard and dying to be inside her.

'Second...option,' she groans.

'Mmm, good girl,' I praise. We're already pressed tightly against each other. I take hold of my thick length and drag it seductively through her ample juices, grateful we've previously had the conversation about contraception. The feeling that the movement creates makes both of us groan throatily with longing. Collecting her mouth with my own, we start to kiss deeply, as I edge myself slowly inside.

I always knew making love to Annie would be incredible, but nothing prepares me for the reality. She's incredibly warm, wet and welcoming as I rock slowly into her, allowing her body time to adjust. It's been some time since either of us has had sex, and I want us to savour every moment of our first time. I refuse to allow pain or discomfort to enter into the equation, so I proceed carefully and tenderly, just like Annie deserves.

When I eventually bottom out, I temporarily still. Unable to cope with the pleasure high, I feel quite dizzy and not entirely in control of my faculties. But I'm not given the option to pause. Annie is proving herself ravenous for more. Instantly, she pulls me hard against her, attempting to rock her hips, even though my weight is largely pinning her to the bed. With a grunt of despair, I start to move, sliding myself slowly in and out, maximising our joint enjoyment while appreciating my actions are swiftly eroding my own self-control.

Thanks to her cries demanding more, I am soon driving myself deep, eyes flickering closed as my cries of anguish combine with her pleasurable ones. I wanted to last a long time, but Annie's amazing mouth has already pushed me to the very limit. I guess it's hardly surprising that I'm back there again within such a short space of time, desperate to come.

'Harder, please. Harder!' she squeals, as I continue to plough myself deep.

In despair, I follow her demands to the letter, even though I appreciate it will result in my own demise. As Annie spirals into yet another incredibly powerful climax, I groan as my fingers dig into her thigh. With the tip of my pulsing cock being driven impossibly deep, nudging against her cervix with each and every thrust, I know I must submit to the inevitable. Feeling Annie tighten considerably around me, coaxing my pleasure even higher, I can hold back no more.

'I'm gonna come,' I grunt, almost instantly spilling my seed with intense relief, my actions accompanied by a deep, rumbling roar that makes my chest vibrate.

For a little while afterwards, we don't say a word. We don't even move. I slowly become aware of our sweating bodies and the way our fast, panting breaths are gradually calming. Stiffly, I lift my head, supporting my weight on precariously shaking limbs. As my eyes meet Annie's, we smile broadly at each other.

'You're amazing,' she sighs, looking as though she's seconds from unconsciousness.

'In which case, you're completely phenomenal,' I admit, easing myself gently out. But I don't articulate the final word correctly. It sounds wrong, but in my confused thoughts, I can't quite untangle it to land on the correct pronunciation. But then it doesn't matter anymore. Within seconds of me collapsing down upon the mattress, I join Annie in an exhausted and much required sleep.

INHALING DEEPLY, I enjoy the scent of the ocean, the fresh, salty air filling my lungs, and the presence of the woman walking beside me, barefoot on the sand. Having woken from our impromptu snooze, we've taken a late afternoon stroll down to the coast. Like children at times, we've splashed in the waves, laughed, smiled, hugged and kissed at every possible opportunity. My heart is brimming over with love and if right now isn't the perfect opportunity to tell Annie how I feel about her, then I don't know when it will be.

'Hey, Annie,' I say gently, causing the edges of her mouth to lift.

'Yeah,' she replies teasingly, looking utterly content with life.

'I love you.' Three simple words, and they couldn't be more accurate.

A look of genuine delight floods her features as she reaches out for me.

'I love you too, Jack. And I always have.' My chest instantly erupts with sensation, my heart beating at twice the normal safe speed. And then our lips join. Not giving a crap that we're surrounded by holidaymakers, we grab onto each other and kiss as though our lives depend upon it. At last, the woman I need is safe in my arms, and I never intend to let her go again.

Having embarrassed ourselves adequately by snogging like two horny teenagers on the sand, Annie and I take a walk around the amusement arcades. Soon, we're focused on a very involved game of air hockey and I quickly discover that Annie cheats! Trying her best to distract me by voicing all kinds of wicked promises across the table, I am soon four-five down, when I should by all accounts be winning. The money runs out of the game, just seconds before I'm primed to deploy the equalising shot. Jubilant in her victory, Annie starts to giggle, quickly discovering that she can't stop. Soon, she's on her knees, holding her aching tummy muscles, tears of laughter rolling down her cheeks. Inhaling deeply, I can only watch in delight. A sense of sheer happiness fills me as I acknowledge that the girl I've been searching for my entire life has returned to me. But, perhaps more importantly, she's returned to herself as well.

EPILOGUE

ANNIE

6 months later

We collapse through the front door with rosy red cheeks aching from smiling too much, and our eyes aglow with excitement. It's the fifth of November and I've just spent an amazing fireworks night with my two favourite guys in the entire world; Tobes and Jack. We've overdosed on funfair rides, toffee apples and candy floss, not to mention enjoying watching the firelight flicker across each other's rapt faces, as the bonfire flames licked towards the dark, starry sky. It's getting late, so I immediately encourage Toby towards the stairs to commence his bedtime routine.

'Goodnight, mate,' grins Jack, affectionately sending my son a playful wink.

'Night, Jack,' he replies, smiling back. Toby gave up calling him *Mr Harrison* months ago, except when they are in class. It was going to get too weird otherwise.

I follow Toby upstairs, but I'm largely surplus to requirements these days. There was a time when I would be needed to assist with bathroom duties, brush Toby's teeth, read a story and ensure there were no scary monsters under the bed. But he can manage all of that by himself now. My little boy is growing up fast; a fact I know I can't deny, however much I might want to. Within a year, I shouldn't be surprised to discover he reaches my shoulders in height. And then where will it end? Before I know it, he'll be towering over me, a huge six foot plus, rugby-playing man. But he'll always be my baby, and the most precious person in my life.

Within no time, I'm returning to the kitchen where Jack is putting the final touches to the hot chocolate he's made us both, by adding some marshmallows. Sharing a warm drink has become a night-time ritual that I'm very fond of, although I wish we didn't have to sleep apart. Since we got together, Jack and I have been spending loads of time together and creating a ton of new memories, but we only physically sleep together when Toby is away for the weekend with his grandparents, or staying at his father's house. But I for one am ready to take the next step although, of course, the situation isn't just about what I want. There are three of us involved here.

'For you, Ma'am,' he says, sliding his creation across the table towards my seat.

'You're too kind,' I smile, as we both sit down.

'So I'm told,' he admits, his eyes twinkling. I know he's joking, but the thing is, it's actually true. Jack is about as perfect as it is possible to be. Ever since we first got together, he's been true to his word, patiently waiting as we gradually introduce Toby to the concept of his mother seeing a new man. Jack has applied absolutely no pressure to the situation, which in so far as I'm concerned, speaks volumes about his calibre as an all-round amazing human being. The only urgency in this situation has been generated by me. Patience has never been my forte and I want my chosen partner in the very centre of my life. But although I am the instigator to move our relationship up to the next level, I'm guessing Jack will be a perfectly willing participant.

'I love you,' I sigh, taking his hand across the table. 'And I want more than this.'

'I love you too,' he replies. It certainly isn't the first time we've shared this sentiment, but I feel completely adored every time I hear Jack say those words. 'How much more do you want?'

'It kills me that we have to say goodbye to each other every night, when all I want to do is hold you until the following morning.'

'You want to live together?' he asks, taking a sip of his hot chocolate and not looking at all freaked out by the suggestion.

'I need you closer. I want to build my life around both you and Toby.' With previous relationships, I'd have been nervous about sharing something that significant, but not with Jack. He's become my closest friend and we are never afraid to share the absolute truth with each other. To be honest, after living through a catalogue of Lee's lies and cheating, it is certainly a very refreshing and welcome approach.

'I'd like that very much,' he admits tenderly, squeezing my hand. 'But this isn't a decision the two of us can make.'

'It isn't?'

'No. Toby has to have a say in this too. He's an integral part of you, so that makes him equally as important for me to love and cherish, but also respect.' I swallow hard as his words impact my heart. If I didn't already realise Jack was the guy for me, I certainly know it now.

'So when can we ask him?' I say enthusiastically, practically having to hold myself back from racing upstairs before Toby falls asleep, so we can finalise the matter now.

'Not *we*. You,' explains Jack. His tone is so serious that it sends a shiver up my spine. I chew my lower lip in response. I love it when he's strict with me. 'As his school teacher, I'm in a position of authority. Toby needs to be given time to process everything, and then give his opinion honestly, without me being present. This is a conversation the two of you need to have alone.'

I pull a face at Jack. Are we seriously allowing my ten-year old to decide upon the fate of our relationship?

'I mean it,' he says, responding to my expression. 'Whatever either of you chooses has my full support. I wasn't lying when I said I'd wait for you, Annie. I'll wait an eternity if I have to. I want more too, eventually, but I'm not willing to fuck around with your son's emotions, in order to further my own happiness. He has to come first in this situation. Agreed?'

'Agreed,' I nod, not bothering to try and hide the tears which have started to flow.

———

THE FOLLOWING MORNING, I'm sitting at the breakfast table drumming up some courage for the conversation I'd like to have, when Toby ambles downstairs. His Superman pyjamas look a little short in the leg and I silently make a note to purchase some new ones.

'Morning, Mum. Where's Jack?' he asks straightaway.

'He's at his house, Sweetheart,' I explain, my heart beating noisily. 'Why do you ask?'

'Why doesn't he ever stay overnight?'

'Well...um...' I stutter.

'Dad has Cynthia over at his house all the time when I stay over.'

Fortunately, Toby is intent on filling his bowl with cereal at this juncture, so he misses the flash of disapproval that passes across my face. Reminding myself it isn't in my son's best interests to snipe about his hopeless father and the multitude of female partners he seems to be working his way through, I bite my tongue and proceed with the conversation I wish to have.

'Wouldn't you mind, then, if Jack stayed overnight?' I ask tentatively.

'Mind?' he smiles, between shovelling cornflakes into his mouth. 'Why would I mind? Jack's the coolest!'

Praise indeed.

'I'm glad you think so, Sweetheart. So you don't find it too strange that Mummy's seeing Mr Harrison? I mean, he is your teacher.'

'I know that, Mum!' Toby replies, with a rather dramatic eye roll. I've recently been noting the shift from calling me Mummy to Mum. My little boy is growing up fast. Maybe he is ready for this, after all.

'It's just, we do love each other very much.'

'Are you going to have another baby?' he asks, quite innocently.

'No, Darling! No, I'm not having a baby,' I reply quickly, instantly able to feel myself blushing. But I know what his logic is based on. A mummy and a daddy loving each other very much has always been the way I've explained procreation to Toby. I guess it's understandable that he might be confused. 'But in time, we would very much like to live together, but only if you're happy for that to happen.'

'Do you think you could ask Jack if he could stay from tonight?' suggests Toby with surprising enthusiasm. 'I'd really like to go fishing with him again. Perhaps we could go this afternoon? And go to the park tomorrow?'

'Er, yes. I suppose.'

'Could you phone him now? Pleeaaase?'

'Sure,' I laugh, as Toby abandons his breakfast mid-spoonful, in order to look out his fishing rods. I don't know what I did to be blessed with my son, but I'm grateful for it every single day.

With a soft smile, I pick up my mobile phone and send Jack a text. In time, we can all share a conversation about us moving in together, but for now, I'm grateful for this special moment. The existence of the two men I love most in my life and their total acceptance of each other. How many people are that lucky? Last night, Jack and I chatted through the logistics of living together, if Toby was amenable. Jack was clear that he didn't want to disrupt Toby's life unnecessarily and suggested that he could move into our home. Jack's house is by far the larger property, but the upheaval of moving could have a negative impact on the one person we have both sworn to protect. In time, perhaps we could purchase somewhere new together, but for now, being a couple and living together here will be more than enough. It is both of our dreams fulfilled. After all, we have the rest of our lives together. Jack was right when he said it; our time is now.

THE END

APOLOGY NOT ACCEPTED

FENELLA ASHWORTH

CHAPTER 1

CARRIE

Subtly attempting to reposition my body for what feels like the hundredth time, I manage to suppress a dramatic eye roll, instead pouring my frustration into exhaling deeply. Through the inadequately narrow window in front of me, I can see the weather outside is magnificent. England at the height of Summer can be incomparable on a good day...and today is obviously one of those. Azure blue skies, peppered with the occasional cotton-wool cloud, a very light warm breeze. It's all there, just waiting to be explored. And instead, I'm stuck inside a glorified shed; hungry, thirsty, desperate for a wee and starting to sweat unattractively, while surrounded by a group of over-enthusiastic ornithologists. Sigh.

Still obeying the silence this apparently hallowed environment allegedly deserves, I glance across at my best friend, Briony. With binoculars pressed to her eyes, she's watching the woodland floor intently. No doubt some fascinating beetle or woodlouse is soon to be lovingly recorded on the clipboard which is balanced on her lap. If only I could summon up the necessary enthusiasm to be equally engaged, but alas, it is too much of an ask.

Needless to say, taking part in the annual wildlife survey at the great Goldingford Park is much more Briony's thing than mine. But being an amazing friend, she insisted that I join her today, in the hopes it might cheer me up. I got dumped a little while back by a guy I'd been seeing. Wanker. It wasn't serious with him and was never going to be, but his rejection still impacted my self-esteem a little harder than expected. Although quite why Briony thought that sitting in a shed for five hours straight was likely to cheer me up, I'll never know. Sorry, not a shed. A *hide*.

As the lead organiser of the event, Briony has worked hard over the past ten years to rally the volunteers and maintain good communications with the landowner, Phillip Lancaster, Duke of somewhere or other. Rich and powerful within the local community, the guy lives in the mansion nearby, surrounded by literally hundreds of acres. The woodland in which we're currently camped out is just one small part of it. It's certainly a world away from my compact, three-bedroomed home with a postage stamp-sized garden, situated in the centre of a nearby village. But there's no point being bitter.

I shuffle in my seat again and try to catch Briony's eye. The situation with my bladder is fast becoming urgent. I didn't have the chance to question her about the lavatory situation upon arrival, but I've seen no sign of any facilities thus far. In an attempt to take the focus off my discomfort, I glance down at the identification chart in front of me. It provides the names and images of some creatures the observers are likely to see, including both a fox and a badger. I huff dramatically; I know practically sod all about wildlife, but even *I'm* capable of identifying those! My eyes slide down to study some of the other birds on the page and my frustration only intensifies. To my uneducated eye, the Grey Wagtail looks more yellow in colour than the Yellow Wagtail does. God, they don't make these things easy, do they?

Suddenly, there's a flurry of activity within the hide, as everybody surrounding me leans closer to the window. I glance in the same direction, only to see the most beautiful fallow deer wander cautiously into the observation area. With the most incredible golden fur, dappled with white spots, its over-large ears and delicate legs have me entranced.

'Wow,' I moan, feasting my eyes on our new visitor. 'You are so beautiful.'

In rapt fascination, I observe the creature as it picks its way carefully across the woodland glade and away. Only when it has departed do I turn towards a beaming Briony; she looks like all her birthdays and Christmases have come at once.

'Wasn't that amazing?' she enthuses, her voice breaking slightly with emotion.

I nod. I honestly don't want to ruin the moment but the situation has turned critical.

'It was,' I agree, beaming back at her, while subtly squeezing my thighs together. 'And I honestly hate to spoil anything...but what happens when you need a wee around here?'

With a giggle, Briony shakes her head at my apparent ineptitude.

'I told you not to drink so much tea at my house!'

'Never mind that now,' I urge. 'Where's the toilet?'

'You're surrounded by woodland,' replies Briony. 'Just exit the hide quietly and then head deeper into the woods to find a suitable spot.'

'Seriously? That's it?' I splutter. 'You expect me to squat beneath a bush?'

'It's either that, or you'll need to wait until we get back home,' my friend explains patiently.

'And how long will that be?'

'A couple of hours?'

'For fuck's sake,' I grumble.

'Oh! Plus, I also need to pop into Goldingford House before we leave. I always like to thank the Duke in person. It's kind of him to permit us here each year, plus it will help ensure he allows us to return in the future. You'll come with me, won't you?'

'Yeah, okay,' I agree. The house isn't open to the public but it's supposed to be the most amazing building. I'm definitely signed up to any activity which will allow me to have a snoop around. 'What's he like?'

'Nice chap... well, for a rich bloke anyway,' Briony corrects with a giggle. 'He's lived here his entire life, so for the past sixty years or so. He's always got a lot of stories to tell.'

'I bet,' I say, rising to my feet. The time has come. 'I'll be back in a bit,' I mutter, before exiting through the door. Instantly, I'm aware of some vague tutting from the other nature enthusiasts, thanks to the increased level of noise I'm subjecting them to. Geez! I swear more noise is permitted inside the British Library than this poky little shed.

Outside, the day is equally as amazing as I'd anticipated it to be. The woodland canopy protects me from the majority of the sun's heat, but glimmers of light still manage to dance across the earthy floor while a cacophony of birdsong fills my ears. Unfortunately I don't have time to pause and enjoy the sylvan scene; there are much more important functions I must attend to.

Stomping away from the hide at speed, I keep glancing back. It's frustrating to discover that no matter how far I walk, at least a corner of the hide always remains in view. Starting to get a bit of a complex, I travel even further into the undergrowth, eventually pausing behind a fallen Oak tree which I decide provides an adequate amount of visual protection for my sensibilities. Taking a final glance around, I quickly unbutton my shorts, pull down the clothing on the lower half of my body and squat with enormous relief.

But my swift moment of solitude is apparently not to be. I'm only half way through my task when I hear a vaguely familiar noise starting to build around me. Glancing around with concern, only at the point my bladder has mercifully been emptied do I realise with horror that the approaching sound is a galloping horse. Still with my shorts around my ankles, I pop my head slightly above the adjacent fallen tree, instantly wishing I hadn't done so. With utter horror, I watch the undercarriage of an enormous bay horse sail almost directly over the top of my head. My natural reaction is to scream, but absolutely no noise comes out of my wide open mouth. Instead, with a squeak which originates deep from within my terrified soul, I instantly duck back down again as the beast lands, thanking my lucky stars that it missed me.

Rising quickly, I secure my clothing and shoot an angry stare towards the irresponsible rider who has just endangered our lives. I may well be in shock, but I quickly recognise that's nothing compared to how the poor horse feels. Having inadvertently leapt over a human being, it is now bucking and rearing just metres away from me, as the rider attempts to regain control of his mount. Against my better judgement, I'm impressed by the stranger for sticking onboard. I've done enough horse riding in my younger years to appreciate this guy must have impressive leg muscles to stay seated on that rodeo ride. The man is a natural-born horseman. I can almost hear the creature groaning as a powerful thigh pressure is applied, to ensure the rider doesn't fall off his steed. Consequently, he barely moves an inch in the saddle.

Eventually, the animal calms, which is more than can be said for me.

'What the *actual* fuck do you think you're doing here?' I explode, fear fuelling my bad temper. As I dare to confront the rider, I look at him properly for the first time. Instantly, the air rushes from my lungs. About my age, perhaps a few years older, he's absolutely gorgeous. Dark tendrils of hair are escaping from beneath his black, velvet riding hat, what I can see of his torso beneath a plain white T-shirt is well-muscled and just as I'd suspected, the powerful legs beneath his skin-tight jodhpurs are exquisite. Totally against my wishes, my internal muscles clench hard, sending a buzz of sexual desire straight through me. Damn him.

'I might ask you exactly the same question,' he replies, his deep voice causing a swirling confusion of attraction, desire and pure animal lust to build inside me. He manages to sound both like a well-brought up English gentleman and a filthy fucker, all at the same time. But I'm not to be distracted...well, not much, anyway.

'*I* am on a data-gathering exercise for the local nature conservancy group, with express permission from the landowner,' I state primly, making my experience of sitting for five hours in a small shed with no toilet facilities sound far more glamorous than it has the right to. '*You* are trespassing, by riding around on private property.'

The fucker dares to look amused by my somewhat aggressive

statement, even displaying the audacity to flash me a smile as his dark eyes flicker down my body.

'I stand corrected and consider myself appropriately reprimanded,' he drawls. 'It has been my pleasure to meet you, Miss...?'

'None of your bloody business!' I snap, feeling unwillingly exposed. There's no way I'm telling this arrogant little fucker my name. But rather than looking angered by my hostility, on the contrary, he continues to smile. I can't help but silently acknowledge that it's a very attractive smile. And that makes sense, given he's an incredibly attractive guy.

'In which case, my sincere apologies for disturbing your er...badger spotting.'

I flush slightly, given we both know he's caught me weeing in the woods. But before I'm given the chance to reply, the man has already spun his horse around and trotted off in the opposite direction. I watch him expertly steer the horse back onto a wider track I hadn't previously noticed. Within a minute, they are both out of sight. Still shaking, I stride back to the hide and take my place beside Briony.

'You've been ages. Are you okay?'

'That's a very personal question,' I joke, sending her a small smile. 'But I'm fine, thanks.'

'So why were you so long?' she presses, oblivious to the fox which has just started to creep into view. I lean over and tap the appropriate box on her clipboard, in the hope it might divert her attention away from me. With limited enthusiasm, she enters a tally of one.

'Just some trouble with the locals,' I mutter, not willing to provide any further details.

CHAPTER 2

RICHARD

A good gallop across country normally manages to clear my head, but not today. My earlier hack out across the estate only made everything seem more confused than ever. And I know exactly why. That woman I bumped into, almost literally, with her gorgeous blonde curls and piercing blue eyes, has set my head in somewhat of a spin. I can't stop thinking about her, almost as though I'm bewitched. Every time I blink, I see her image behind my eyelids, as though she's been burnt into my memory. I would say my soul, but that sounds far too melodramatic and I'm not that kind of guy.

I'm also typically not the kind of guy that people refuse to comply with. When I ask for someone's name, that person almost always obliges. Obviously the woman had no idea who I was when she said...what was it? None of your bloody business? I'm not sure if it's her obstinate reaction which has ended up intriguing me so, but I can't deny that she has me interested. She has me very interested indeed. I just need to track her down now and find out who the hell she is.

'Are you ready to eat, Sir?' The mild voice of one of our house-maids doesn't begin to compare with the combative tones I was subjected to earlier.

'Yes, thank you Hopkins,' I reply with a brief nod. 'I'll take lunch out in the garden.'

Strolling through the huge, somewhat imposing corridors, I make my way to the back of the house and step outside. Instantly, the warm Summer's day offers a stark contrast to the cool, refined air I'd been enjoying. The midday sun is really pitching down now, so I stroll across our beautifully maintained lawns towards the orchard, to sit beneath the apple trees which are swaying gently overhead. Taking a deep breath, I settle down in a comfortable chair and stretch my feet in front of me. And there I sit, thinking and brooding about that mysterious woman until my lunch is served.

Although the selection of antipasto is relatively straightforward, it is exquisitely produced and presented. The new chef we've employed was hired on the understanding he was first class, but it's nice to have early evidence to back up his claims and references. It's probably just as well he meets the required standard because my father has organised yet another banquet next week. The purpose of this one is to impress Lady Catherine and her three good-natured but dreary daughters. If I'm being forced to endure a long, tedious evening in their company, I will certainly appreciate it being accompanied by decent food.

I have no doubt that my father's sudden interest in hosting a banquet for Lady Catherine is in the desperate hope that I might marry one of her offspring. Knowing my father, he'll probably rope my poor, unsuspecting younger brother in too, and attempt to marry off two of his sons for the price of one. I'm probably being vastly unfair; the three daughters are pleasant enough in their own way, but they're a product of our upbringing and social class. I already know that a well brought up, docile lady who refuses to challenge the status quo isn't for me. Besides, what the hell do I want with a Lady?

Alas, my father is proving himself increasingly keen to marry me off, no doubt to ensure the line of succession for our great and ancient family name, continues on into the future. A personal achievement that he can find comfort in as he grows older. As the eldest son, I certainly feel the pressure of his expectations. But unfortunately for my father, I'm not willing to sacrifice my own needs and happiness, simply to settle down faster than I'm ready to do, with a girl he deems suitable. And to be quite honest, I find it increasingly frustrating that he continues to throw rich, eligible young women at me, as if a pretty face and a pile of cash is all it takes. Indeed, I find the implication rather insulting.

Even I know that true attraction requires so much more than that. I want a life partner and an equal. Somebody to share joy, tears and elation with. Somebody who is on my wavelength, with a shared sense of humour and a mind of her own. And unlike your bog-standard debutante, I'm becoming painfully aware that is a whole lot more difficult to come by. In fact, I'm starting to fear that it might be an impossible ask.

Pushing aside my empty plate, I inhale deeply, loving the feel of the dappled sun flickering over the exposed skin of my arms and face. Angling the chair backwards, I close my eyes and relax. The truth of the matter is that, however difficult it might end up being to find her, I would like someone I can share this with. I can't deny that I live a blessed life, but it can be a lonely one. And I fear that as I grow older, I am also growing more difficult to please...more particular and set in my ways. Increasingly, I know that the person I eventually do end up with will have to be one hell of a woman; certainly nobody I've ever met within my social circles could fill such large boots.

Now that I'm warm, content and well-fed, the woman I met earlier in the woods dares to float back into my subconscious thoughts. I must have dozed off to sleep, because the next thing I know, I'm being woken by the soft but insistent voice of our maid.

'Begging your pardon, Sir, but your father would like you to join him in the yellow drawing room.'

With a grunt, I unwillingly open my eyes and glance at my watch, while Hopkins tidies away my plate.

'Any idea why?' I grumble, rising to my feet to tower over the woman.

'None at all, I'm afraid, Sir.'

Thrusting my hands into the deep pockets of my jeans, I stride across the lawn and duck back inside the great house. It's dark and cool here, immediately ensuring that I dispense with my sunglasses. The door of the yellow drawing room is open when I approach it and I can hear the chattering of conversation taking place from within. Stepping assuredly inside, the very first thing I see is her mass of blonde curls and my chest expands almost painfully. She's here. I've found her. Thank God! My brain is screaming out in rejoice, while my heart thumps loudly throughout my body. Just as I remember, the girl is striking in the extreme. The first time we met, I thought I might have been suffering from an adrenaline high, thanks to the near miss I'd had on my horse. Thinking back, I'm no longer confident that was the reason I couldn't breathe properly. But despite the shock, I somehow manage to ignore my racing pulse and stroll confidently across the room to stand beside my father, working hard to ensure my expression remains neutral.

'Ah! Richard!' he exclaims, looking delighted by my arrival. 'Ladies, may I introduce my son, Richard, Earl of Winchester.'

I watch the woman look directly up at me. In slow motion, her jaw becomes slack as her mouth falls open in shock. Her face is an absolute picture. I only wish I had some kind of recording device to capture the occasion. Her horror at realising she's recently screamed and hollered accusations of trespass at the very man who's in line to inherit the entire estate, really is sublime. Honestly, I'm trying my hardest not to laugh but it is a struggle. I don't think my father has noticed the undercurrents which are rippling between us though, instead electing to plough on with the introductions regardless.

'Richard, this is Miss Briony Walters who organises the annual wildlife survey that takes place on the estate?'

'A pleasure to meet you,' I say, accompanying the act of shaking her hand with a brief nod of my head.

'And this is her friend and accomplice, Miss...'

'Don't tell me,' I interrupt. For as much as I'd love to know this woman's name, my urge to tease her is even greater. 'We've already met. *Miss None Of Your Bloody Business*, wasn't it?'

Amused that she is now visibly cringing, I hold out my hand, unsurprised by the zing of desire that shoots through my arm and into my chest, as skin touches skin for the very first time. I get the distinct feeling that something similar is taking place within her body too. She certainly inhales sharply, and the longer I claim possession of her hand, the deeper she appears to be blushing. Could she be any more adorable? God, if she blushes this easily, I can't help imagining how she'll react when confronted with the truth about all the wicked things I want to do to her.

'Carrie,' she croaks, sounding like her vocal chords have forgotten how to function.

I smile gently. There it is. Carrie. A beautiful name which certainly suits her.

'My pleasure, Carrie,' I grunt. There's obviously something contagious going around because now I'm struggling to speak properly too. 'How goes the badger spotting?'

'It was a very successful day, thank you,' Briony answers after an embarrassingly long pause. She's obviously realised her friend isn't in a position to respond.

I know I should release her hand at some point, but neither of us seems inclined to do so. It's strange because I've been taking part in extreme activities for so long, simply as a way to *feel* something. But I can't ever remember anything providing me with the kind of rush I'm experiencing right now. Horse racing, rock climbing, bungee jumps, motocross, parachuting...I've done it all. But nothing has ever given me the thrill I'm experiencing from being with this woman, in this moment. And right now, that sensation is almost too much. This is what I've been missing out on. *This* is the buzz I've been searching for, for longer than I dare to remember.

I'm thrilled when she discovers her voice at last.

'I believe I owe you an apology.'

'I believe you do,' I agree, still holding her warm hand in my own larger one.

'I'm sorry for shouting at you, when you were riding across your own land,' she says quietly. I nod with encouragement, before deciding to turn the tables on her. Right now, I have Carrie at a disadvantage. I'm not normally one to play mind games, but this situation definitely warrants being approached with the precision of a chess grandmaster. Played correctly, I might just get what I want...and what I believe, deep down, we both want. Right now, she's in my debt. And I intend to keep her there for as long as possible. So although my response goes against my normal good manners and upbringing, with a straight face I square my shoulders and look her directly in the eye.

'Apology *not* accepted.'

CHAPTER 3

CARRIE

'I beg your pardon?' I explode, instinctively snatching my hand away from his. I won't deny that the zing of Richard's touch was incredibly enjoyable, but I have minimum standards and I intend to maintain them.

'You heard me...apology not accepted.'

'I...but...' I stammer hopelessly in response. Refusing to accept an apology is not the way people treat each other...especially well brought up, decent people, which I thought this man was.

'Richard...' his father gently reprimands, suggesting that he supports my point of view.

But this *Richard*, Earl of wherever it was, is apparently in no mood to yield.

'You used to ride?' he asks me in a rather direct fashion. He's unafraid to look me straight in the eye, and I suppress a small shiver of longing and raise my chin insolently. He's even taller than I'd suspected when I first saw him on horseback. I'm not exactly short myself, but he's got to be six foot two...six foot three perhaps? I always think that's a very nice height.

Good Lord! What is wrong with me today? A nice height for what?!

'I did used to ride,' I confirm, trying to keep my tone neutral, despite my wild, runaway thoughts. 'How did you know?'

'It isn't difficult to tell.'

I'm not entirely sure what to make of that statement. Of course, he's correct that I once used to horse ride very regularly. It was one of the great joys and loves of my life, in fact. I haven't done it for years, although with a slightly fat ass, and my hair pulled back into a pony-tail, I reluctantly have to accept the clues are probably there. Or maybe I'm being too harsh on myself. Maybe Richard observed how I barely reacted when his horse was pirouetting in front of me earlier, remaining calm and simply holding out an arm whenever it pranced too close for comfort.

'I require a groom for the charity point to point race I'm riding in next weekend,' he announces. 'Undertake that role for me and your apology will be accepted.'

I know the exact event he's referring to; a local horse race over what my grandfather would have referred to as "the sticks"; basically, two loops of a field up the road, with horse and rider required to successfully jump a number of obstacles. Kind of like the poor man's Grand National, although of course, there is nothing poor about this man.

'And if I refuse?' Naturally defiant, I instantly snap back. To be honest, I'm not sure whether to be angry or amused by his offer, although I admit to being subconsciously eased into the latter frame of mind, thanks to both the sound of Briony giggling, and the way Richard's eyes crinkled softly at the corners when he spoke. But still, I refuse to be pushed around, even by an Earl.

'Then I won't accept your apology,' he explains, his tone remaining playful.

'I'm failing to see how that's my problem,' I admit, trying to contain an escaping smile. 'Why should I care whether my apology is accepted by you, or not?'

'Ordinarily, of course, you wouldn't. But I'm not just offering a day for you to toil as my groom. I'm also offering you a treat afterwards, to say thank you.'

This time, I can't help it. The laughter erupts from me, before I'm given the option of controlling it. My conversation with Richard is taking up all of my focus but still, I'm aware we are not the only two people in the room. I quickly sneak a glance at Briony, who grins back at me, looking thoroughly pleased at this turn of events. Feeling bolstered, I return my attention to Richard.

'Oh yeah? And what treat is that?'

'An early dinner, before accompanying you to a rather large event which is taking place at Blenworth Estate later that same evening.'

'Seriously?' I stutter. I think he's referring to the charity rock concert, at which some of my biggest childhood heroes are scheduled to be playing. The huge outdoor event has been the talk of the local community for months now, even though tickets sold out almost as soon as they went on sale. 'You don't really strike me as the kind of person who enjoys rock music.'

'Is that right?' Richard enquires, one eyebrow raising in such a suggestively sexy way, that it instantly feels like a swarm of inebriated butterflies have taken control of my tummy. 'Well, you know what they say? Never judge a book by its cover. So? Will you accept *my* offer, in order that I might accept *your* apology?'

Continuing to smile, I chance another look at Briony who is positively beaming. We exchange a glance which says more than words ever could. I can instinctively tell that Briony is encouraging me to accept his offer, and I silently admit that she kind of has a point. Richard seems like a very decent, very sexy guy who likes me enough that he's willing to flirt in front of his own father.

'Go on,' Briony mouths, urging me to accept. But before I provide my response, Richard's father steps in, in defence of his son.

'I think, in a very slapdash, ambiguous and clumsy way, my son is attempting to romance you,' explains the Duke.

'By making me work as his groom? Seriously?' I complain, my brow scrunching up in disbelief.

'Like I said, slapdash, ambiguous and clumsy,' he shrugs. 'I think he's forgotten how to treat a lady.'

'Um, excuse me? I am still here, you know?' complains Richard.

'I'm standing here in the room, *right* beside you. Right now. Can you even see me?'

Such is the comedic indignation of his reaction that I start to giggle. But the moment I catch his gaze once more, the heat starts to rise from within and I wish I hadn't dared to look at him. The natural connection between us has the potential to become electric, very fast indeed. Ignoring his son, the Duke continues.

'Please do consider it, my dear? If not for him, then for me? I've been trying for years to identify a suitable date for my ridiculously picky first born. Every woman I've ever suggested, he's refused, and I've been disinclined to approve of the women he has brought home. I do believe you're the only girl I've ever met that we both like!'

My eyes slide back towards Richard and his gently reddening cheeks. Immediately I know his father is speaking the truth. Suddenly, I'm taken back to my school days, as a Venn diagram image appears in my mind. One circle is labelled Richard, the other is labelled Phillip, and I'm dancing a solitary jig where the two circles interlink.

'Fine!' I huff, sending Richard a small shrug to suggest that the day he has planned for us is of little consequence to me. 'But only because this is the one way I can get to see a rock concert, which I've previously tried and failed to get tickets for.'

'Mmmm, defiant and unafraid of my apparent standing in society,' he murmurs, his voice so low and intimate that I'm pretty confident I'm the only person in the room who can hear him. 'Just the kind of attitude I admire. I find myself both equally captivated and yearning to dispense discipline.'

I try to ignore the mild sexual overtones in his admission but it's impossible to do so. I have no doubt that he means exactly what I think he does. Fortunately, or not, both his father and Briony have missed this little exchange. Feeling the heat rising along my neck and chest, I clear my throat a little shakily and stare back into his wickedly dancing eyes, as rebellious as ever.

'I advise that you just stick with being captivated,' I state, flashing my eyes at him challengingly.

'I will...for now,' he confirms, the qualification said in such a way that it makes my racing pulse speed up further. 'Speaking of which, I would very much like to show you around the stables so you're prepared. Might you have a little spare time now?'

'Er?' I glance towards my friend for her opinion. After all, we did travel here in her car.

'Oh no! I'm really sorry,' mumbles Briony, genuinely looking it. 'But I need to get home very soon; I've got an engagement I mustn't miss.' I smirk at the way my dear friend is unexpectedly acting like an extra on the set of Downton Abbey. I've never heard a visit from the washing machine repair guy described as an *engagement* before, but each to their own.

'Briony is my designated driver,' I explain, in order to help clear Richard's confused expression.

'Ah, well, I'm quite happy to run you back home afterwards,' he offers, easily resolving the potential issue. 'What do you say, Carrie? Do you trust me?' Once again, I feel the full weight of his focus upon me. As I process his words, I can feel my tummy turning all squirmy.

'Not as far as I can throw you,' I joke, making everyone in the room chuckle. But he is apparently not to be distracted, continuing to watch me carefully until I provide what he obviously deems is an appropriate answer.

'Fine, if you insist,' I eventually huff, throwing my arms into the air in mock exasperation. The man might well be the hottest thing on two legs that I've ever seen in my life, but that doesn't mean I'm going to roll over and play dead. Nor am I going to bow to his implied superiority, like I don't doubt many women have done before. The great Richard, Earl of Whatsaname has a fight on his hands if he thinks I'm going to be the pushover he first anticipated. Bowing and scraping is not in my genes. Although, talking about jeans, the way his hug that delectable ass, along with other even more interesting parts of his body, is nothing short of sublime.

Suddenly, I feel my cheeks start to glow, in response to my lewd thoughts. Refusing to glance back towards Richard, just in case he can read my desire, I look across to Briony, knowing I'll receive some increasingly necessary moral support.

'If that's okay with you?' I ask her.

'More than okay,' she grins, going so far as to send me a wink. Hmph! So much for moral support!

CHAPTER 4

RICHARD

Feeling strangely apprehensive, I lead Carrie across the wide, sweeping lawns towards the stables. I really want her to like my home; for some reason, her approval means an awful lot to me. Fortunately, the weather is on my side. When the clouds and rain hold off like today, a glorious English summer's day is pretty much unbeatable. As we walk beneath a line of swaying Silver Birch trees which offer us welcome shade as protection from the overhead sun, we occasionally glance across at each other, sharing a small smile. Away from company, the easy, cheeky rapport that had been building has sadly diminished. It was certainly much easier to be playful back at the house. Being alone together in the garden feels a lot more intimate and I don't want to put a foot wrong, as though I recognise the potential importance of our situation. I get the impression that Carrie's as nervous as I am, which provides a little comfort.

'How long have you lived here?' she asks, obviously attempting to break the silence by making conversation.

'Er, all my life,' I reply. I don't mean to sound uncertain, but I'm not sure whether Carrie is asking about me personally, or my family. Because the truth is that the Lancaster family have lived on this land for over five centuries, but admitting that sounds somewhat boastful...pompous even. And that's truly not the kind of person I am.

'And how long's that?' she asks, flashing me a grin which instantly raises my pulse. Ah good, we're returning to gently teasing each other again. About time.

'Are you asking how old I am?'

'Might be,' she giggles, the sound instantly warming my chest.

'And why would you want to know that?' I ask, raising a solitary eyebrow in her direction, silently inhaling with relief that our easy rapport has returned.

'Stop trying to embarrass me!'

'And why would that embarrass you?' I chuckle, before relenting. 'I've lived on Planet Earth for thirty-five years.'

'And before that?' she smirks. But I refuse to let her get away that easily.

'How about you?'

'I do hope you aren't asking a lady her age?'

The instant retort that springs to mind is to jokingly imply that I'm not aware of a lady being present. I'm pretty confident that Carrie's sense of humour matches mine closely enough that she'd find my implication amusing, but it's too soon to risk. She needs to be confident that I consider her a very beautiful lady first, before joking that she isn't one, so instead I simply shrug. The truth is, I don't actually care what her age is. These things don't particularly bother me, although I can tell we aren't so many years apart. Fortunately, the conversational cul-de-sac we're in danger of becoming trapped in is avoided as we reach the stables.

'Well, here we are,' I announce, somewhat redundantly.

'Oh my goodness! What an immaculately kept yard!' she gasps, and there is such sincerity in her voice that I know she speaks the truth. My heart knows it too; I can feel it expanding in my chest with every passing second.

'Thank you,' I reply softly. The stable yard is one of the areas of the house and grounds that I'm solely responsible for and I've always believed in keeping animals in the best possible surroundings and condition. For that reason, not only is it kept clean and tidy, but I've added some touches to make it aesthetically pleasing too. The freshly painted fencing definitely helps to improve the overall view, but I'm still questioning my judgement where the hanging baskets are concerned. Yes, the baskets of brightly coloured flowers hanging from the stable roof are visually appealing, but they are also pretty appealing to the greedy horses too, who constantly attempt to snatch up mouthfuls of the blooms every time they are led past.

'Oh! Hello gorgeous!' Carrie exclaims, causing the breath to momentarily catch in my throat. I instantly feel a sense of disappoint-ment when I realise she isn't talking to me. Approaching the horse's head, which is already hanging over the stable door to ascertain the source of the disturbance, Carrie gently starts to stroke his soft, velvety muzzle. Naturally, the animal pushes back against her, searching for treats. Watching her hands caressing him smoothly, I try my absolute hardest not to feel jealous of a horse. After all, it really isn't the coolest thing in the world to admit to.

'This is Freddie,' I explain, by way of introduction. 'His show name is Alfred the Great.'

'Ah, so not conceited at all then? That's good,' she giggles, flashing her eyes at me once again.

'What would you have chosen?' I enquire, trying to hide my amusement at her bare-faced cheek.

'Something a bit more simple...perhaps just miss off *"the great"* at the end?'

'Hmph,' I grunt, failing to think up a suitable comeback. 'Well, he's the horse I'm racing next Saturday, so I'm very happy to discover you get on so well.'

'Getting on with animals has never been an issue for me,' sighs Carrie, looking as though she's receiving as much pleasure from stroking Freddie as he is. 'It's humans that represent more of a problem.'

Spontaneous laughter escapes from my chest before I realise what's happening, because the truth is, that's exactly how I feel. On the whole, I'd much rather spend my day in the company of animals than people, although I do believe Carrie could be the one human being who might prove themselves to be the exception to that rule.

'Either way, I think Freddie's fantastic,' she continues with obvious admiration. 'What is he? Sixteen hands?'

'Yeah, sixteen three actually. He's a big lad but a real softie.'

'I can tell that,' she smiles, her hand moving to scratch behind his long, pointed ears. 'And he's a very lucky chap to live in such a clean and beautiful environment.'

'Thank you. I agree that my guys do a good job,' I reply, accepting the compliment on their behalf. The truth is, I'm probably a hard taskmaster, but they get paid and treated well for their troubles and don't seem to mind too much...or at least, if they do, they don't tell me.

'Your *guys?*' balks Carrie, immediately making it obvious that I've dropped myself right in it. Bollocks. Although I might as well be honest now.

'Yes,' I admit. 'I've got a full time groom, plus two others that double up as grounds staff.'

'It sounds as though you're already extremely well catered for, in terms of available staff to accompany you to the race?' she observes curtly. 'Which begs the question, what do you need me for?'

I look directly at her, as her bright blue eyes narrow slightly, watching me with suspicion. Hell, I've had quite enough of this tiptoeing around each other.

'I'd have thought that was blatantly obvious Carrie, wouldn't you?'

I'm enchanted to hear her breath catch in her throat, as a gentle flush starts to spread across her neck and cheeks. Yeah, she knows. But still, a defiant gaze flashes back in my direction, confirming that she'll never be a pushover. Instantly I feel a growing pressure in my groin. It's proof, if any were seriously required, of how much I desire this woman. Instinctively, I thrust my hands deep into the pockets of my jeans to hide the physical reaction that I suspect her attitude will shortly cause. This woman excites me more than I probably dare to admit, in a way no other has done before. I know I mustn't overplay my hand but spending a whole day in her company will be like a fantasy come true. Next Saturday literally can't arrive fast enough, in so far as I'm concerned.

We spend a happy few minutes strolling around the yard, as I show her the stables, the barn, the tack room and feed room; in short, everything she'll require when she looks after Freddie next weekend. By the time the tour is complete, my mind is on overdrive, trying to think up an excuse to get her to stay longer today. The truth is, I can't remember enjoying myself this much for years. A multitude of potential excuses race through my mind, guaranteed to elongate her stay... my car has broken down... I feel dizzy... I've got to attend to an emergency...the dog ate my homework. But in the end, given that being honest worked so well before, I decide to just come straight out with it and bare my soul. After all, if she doesn't want me like I want her, it's best to know up front, isn't it? In my opinion, that has to be better than living in hope, where no hope exists.

'Hey, Carrie,' I say gently, causing her gaze to return to me. Suddenly I feel infinitely more nervous.

'Yeah?'

'I'm really enjoying spending time with you. So much, in fact, that I'm not ready for it to end yet. Can we... maybe... go and get something to eat?'

Fine. So it wasn't smooth and it certainly wasn't cool, but it was from the heart. And judging by the way her eyes soften as she processes my words, I get the impression that means a whole lot more.

CHAPTER 5

CARRIE

As the sun begins to sink lower in the sky, I push my bare feet into the soft, warm sand, appreciating that I'm filled with a sense of enormous contentment. Sitting beside each other, Richard and I are looking straight out to sea as evening descends. All around us is the sound of activity; music playing at the funfair on a distant pier, nearby dog walkers, the excited laughter of children who are gradually tiring after a busy day at the beach. But somehow, it feels as though we are the only two people truly present.

'Thank you so much for this,' I say, my words accompanied by a long, relaxing sigh. 'This was such a kind thing to offer.'

'It was entirely selfishly done, I can assure you,' Richard admits gently. 'Kindness had very little to do with it.'

Failing to respond, I return my gaze downwards and pick at the last pieces of fish and chips which are sitting in vinegar-soaked paper on my lap. A fish and chip supper eaten on the beach somehow takes me fleetingly back to my own childhood. The sights and sounds help strengthen my memories as I reminisce; squawking seagulls, gently lapping waves and the failed attempts of the sandcastles we've made surrounding us. As a child, the beach always gave me the sense of freedom and excitement which, strangely enough, is exactly how I feel when I'm with Richard. The hope of what might follow, perhaps? The excitement of the unknown?

'I have to admit, I thought you'd be more of a posh restaurant-loving, food snob kind of guy,' I smile, before taking a swig from the can of fizzy drink which I've pushed into the sand to prevent it from falling over. 'Although I'm thrilled to discover that you're not,' I add quickly, as his face falls. I'd hate him to think I'm disappointed by his choice in any way. As I screw up the empty paper in my hand and turn around to face him, I can't deny that this method of relaxed, informal eating is certainly my preference.

'Will you pleeeeeeeease stop casting your assumptions on me in this provocative manner!' he huffs, failing to hide the smile which is starting to dominate his handsome features. 'What are you basing that opinion on anyway?'

'You've got money,' I shrug. In my experience, if people have money, they tend to want to spend money.

'Yes. And?' he demands playfully. Part of me is impressed that he doesn't try to downplay his wealth although I guess he'd struggle to, given he lives in a veritable mansion. 'So that automatically makes me a snob, right?'

'Noooooooo,' I say quickly, looking guilty because he's hit the nail on the head. My reaction practically answers his question in the affirmative without any further words needing to be spoken.

'Please,' he grins, instantly letting me off the hook.

'The prejudices are strong with this one, right?' I offer, in a poor attempt to recreate a Star Wars line. At least it makes him laugh.

'You're forgiven. Everybody has prejudices, whether you want them or not. It's quite natural.'

'Oh yeah?' I enquire, rising to the bait. 'What are your prejudices about me then?'

Richard studies me carefully and I find myself unable to escape his dark, hungry gaze. It forces the blood to descend from my brain, straight down to my abdomen, leaving me feeling both lightheaded and intensely carnal. I can feel a light tingling sensation in my fingers as I fight the urge to reach across the few inches that separates us, and touch the delectable man sitting so very close by.

'You really want me to answer that?' he asks, the low tone of his voice doing nothing to help quell my swirling desire.

'Yeah, actually I do,' is my immediate reply. I'm forever defiant outwardly, even if inwardly I'm being turned to mush, with every additional minute spent in his company.

'Very well,' he agrees with a small smile. 'But remember; you asked for this.'

Oh God. Now I'm honestly not sure if I want to hear what he's got to say. Then I realise it's too late; he's already started talking.

'I'd have to say my prejudices about you are that you're kind and loving. Responsive...sensitive,' he clarifies, leaving me wondering whether he's talking about my mental or physical state. To be honest, at this point, probably both are true. Part of me hopes he's finished, but then he opens his mouth to deal the killer blow. 'And that you'd kiss like an angel.'

Fuck. So I'm not alone in wondering what it would be like for us to kiss. Somehow, I find that knowledge incredibly reassuring.

'Well, I...' I start, with absolutely zero idea of how the sentence will be ending. 'I'm not sure you should be thinking about my kissing skills!'

'Should I not?' he smiles affectionately. 'In that case, I apologise unreservedly. Now, are you sure you're willing to be my groom on Saturday? On reflection, I do wonder if I've rather railroaded you into it?'

I'm grateful for the change of conversational direction. Indeed, Richard has just demonstrated why I'm growing to like him more and more, with every passing hour we spend together. He's naturally very playful, inquisitive, sexy and challenging, but he never wants me to be uncomfortable. The second he thinks that might be the case, he swiftly removes any pressure, to ensure I don't feel embarrassment or shame.

'I'm more than willing to help you on Saturday,' I admit. 'The truth is, being at your stables earlier reminded me just how much I enjoy being around horses. In my youth, I spent every spare second riding, and I'd forgotten how much I miss that life; the freedom, the pleasure, and the joy of bonding with such magnificent animals.'

Perhaps if money and life allowed, I might try to incorporate horses back into my life again. Something gives me the impression that it would increase my levels of general happiness immensely. Certainly I can't remember, at least within recent years, enjoying myself as much as I have today. But it was invariably much easier to find the time as a child. As an adult, I have various responsibilities to consider first, most of which concentrate around ensuring I have enough money to support myself.

'Well, at the risk of sounding overly keen for it to happen, you are welcome at my stables any time you wish.'

'What, to act as your groom?' I enquire teasingly.

'No, to ride,' he replies, sounding incredibly genuine. 'My stables are yours to use as you wish. I'd love to go out riding with you one day.'

'Thank you, Richard,' I say, with a small nod. 'That means a great deal.'

'You're very welcome. Now, you don't need to get back home yet, do you? Would you join me for a drink?'

'Why are you doing this?' I ask. I probably sound suspicious but I don't care. The guy is a God. A rich God at that. I'm sure he has his pick of any number of incredible women, so I have to wonder what he's doing spending his time attempting to woo scruffy, ordinary and comparatively dishevelled old me.

'Because I'm unwilling to allow our time together to end just yet,' he admits, rising to his feet and then bending down to offer out his hand. Accepting him, our skin inevitably joins and I feel an unexpected zing racing up my arm to prickle against the back of my neck, setting my senses on red alert. I'd suspected it, but now I know for sure. This man does something to me on a subconscious level which I have no control over. And the truth is, I'm more than okay with that.

'Well, you *are* going to see me on Saturday,' I explain, as practical as ever.

'I certainly hope so,' he replies, picking up the litter from both of our dinners, before offering me his spare arm to hold.

As we make our way across the deep sand, our feet struggling to gain a grip, I hold on tightly, appreciating the feel of his powerful arm held within mine. God, the guy's body is unarguably divine.

'What time do you need me to arrive at the stables on Saturday anyway? It had better not be too Early,' I chuckle, amused at my own joke. 'Get it? Earl-ie?'

Thinking about it, being an Earl, my joke probably isn't hugely original for Richard, but he laughs along good-naturedly all the same. Besides, something gives me the impression that everyone probably takes Richard a little too seriously; it's good for him to be brought down a peg or two.

'I do believe that your sense of humour is almost as bad as my father's,' he admits. 'I should probably start running away right now.'

'Well, I thought your dad was great, so I'll take that as a back-handed compliment!'

'Feel free to take my comments however you wish, although on this occasion, I think you're probably being overly generous with your assumptions,' he smirks. 'As for timings, I was actually going to offer to pick you up on Saturday.'

'Really?' I enquire, my nose wrinkling up in surprise. 'Aren't I supposed to be working for you?'

'Actually, I prefer to see it as a symbiotic relationship.'

'I bet you do!' I retort, finding this admission far more amusing than it was probably meant. Why do I feel so damn lighthearted in this guy's company? As we leave the beach and start to make our way along the promenade, it feels as though a magic sparkle has been sprinkled across everything that surrounds us. Long gone is the tired seaside town. Instead, it has been replaced by a scene filled with wonder, enjoyment and immense possibility.

'I'm serious. You're doing me a big favour. The least I can do is drive. Then, if you want to enjoy a few drinks later that evening, you're free to do so.'

'Well, how enormously thoughtful, thank you,' I reply playfully.

Richard squeezes my arm against his in response. 'But you still haven't told me what time you need me to be ready by.'

'Well, I'm in the midday race. Is half past six too early?' he asks, before jokingly adding. 'If it is, perhaps I could come over at that time anyway. Then I could lie in bed beside you until you're ready to er... get up.'

A snort of laughter escapes me, as I shake my head in faux disbelief. The banter is really ramping up now and I have to confess that I love it.

'I'm *appalled* by your lewd suggestions, Sir. What did your last slave die of? Innuendo?'

'So you see yourself as my slave, do you?' Richard queries, flashing me the sexiest look that concurrently sends my stomach plummeting to the ground and whips the breath from my lungs. I instantly realise I've waded way out of my depth. I stare up at him in disbelief, to encounter a twinkle in his eye which confirms that thoughts of a sexual nature are currently lurking just beneath the surface. But as I become overwhelmed by the rising tide of embarrassment, he saves me once again.

'This is a nice bar. Shall we have a drink here?'

CHAPTER 6

RICHARD

I'm not surprised but Carrie and I have a great time down at the coast. Our conversation is interspersed with jokes and laughter, along with the occasionally more serious subject, as we enjoy a number of drinks while becoming increasingly better acquainted with each other. And I can't deny that I *seriously* like what I see. I also feel more at ease than on any previous date. I think it's because I instinctively appreciate that flashing the cash isn't going to impress Carrie; a fact that only makes me desire her more than ever. But that simple fact is allowing me to just be myself and act entirely naturally, without trying to put on an act. I'm finding it very refreshing; freeing almost.

'So let me just get this right,' Carrie requests, fixing me with a playful stare. I raise my eyebrows seductively at her, noticing that she doesn't blush when I confront her directly this time. It's either the effects of the alcohol, or I'm losing my touch.

'Is it *really* the case that you're so hopeless with the opposite sex, you've had to resort to your father setting you up on dates?' she teases, looking delighted by her own daring. Her grin only spreads further when I chuckle in response.

Carrie's observation isn't entirely fair. The truth is, I've never had any trouble finding a woman to date; it's the part that follows which is the issue for me. I want to have a true connection with an equal; somebody I naturally click with, sharing hopes, humour and dreams. I've never met someone I want to screw as much as I want to stay up all night with, just cuddling and chatting. Until today. But I have to admit that Carrie is looking suspiciously like the whole package. Not that she needs to know that, of course, so instead, I decide to just go with her assumption.

'Yeah, something like that,' I reply, simply. 'And how about you? Are you single?'

I try to keep the hope out of my voice, but still my tone rises towards the end of the sentence. The truth is, it's a question I've been dreading asking all day. Of course I want her to confirm that she is single. It would be beyond disappointing to discover that she could flirt this openly with me, while being in a relationship with another guy. I fear it would break the spell she's woven around my heart because she'd no longer be the person I thought she was.

'Yes, I'm single,' she confirms. I completely fail to hide my smile when I hear those words. 'Hey! Don't look quite so happy about it!'

'I don't mean to look happy. Just surprised you haven't been snapped up, I guess.'

'I was going out with a guy a little while ago,' she admits. 'But it didn't work out.

'Oh, I'm sorry,' I say, attempting to look sympathetic, but clearly failing on every level. Carrie can already see straight through me.

'You don't look it,' she observes.

'I don't feel it,' I admit with a guilty smile. 'What happened?'

'He met someone else.'

'Hmmm, well that's all I need to know.' I can already tell the bloke must be a *complete* wanker. I mean, who in their right mind would leave this glorious woman? Clinical insanity would be his only form of defence.

'How do you mean?' she asks.

'He's a knob,' I say frankly, combining my look of distaste with a small shrug. 'If he couldn't see what was right in front of him then he didn't deserve you.' Again, her eyes drop down to the table. Naturally,

I reach across and squeeze her warm, soft fingers, silently marvelling at how my hand completely encompasses hers. Swallowing down a surge of desire, I watch her eyes rise back up to meet mine, her teeth chewing gently on her bottom lip. God, how I wish it was my mouth stimulating that lip instead.

'Well, thank you for your support, but it does still hit your self-confidence, you know?' she says with unusual seriousness.

'Yeah, I know.'

'Anyway, you're quite right. He is a knob!' she agrees, a smile cracking her face once more and restoring equilibrium to the world again, or at least to *my* world. 'And as we're on the subject, he's in possession of a very small knob. And it's slightly crooked too!'

'How very unfortunate,' I grin, as Carrie opens her mouth in shock, as though she can't quite believe she's admitted as much. Suddenly, we are both giggling. Then, just like a snowball effect, no matter how much we try and stop, it just gets worse. With my hands grasping onto my aching abs, I am soon gasping for breath alongside Carrie. And then I realise with unexpected clarity, that the last time I laughed this hard was with my brother when we were both still kids. Duty and adult worries have silenced my inner child over the decades, but that is apparently no longer the case. Thanks to Carrie, the playful version of myself is back out and overflowing with life and mischief. Eventually, we get to the hiccupping stage, taking long deep breaths in an attempt to steady ourselves.

'Oh my God! I'm *so* sorry! Please forget I ever said that!' Carrie requests, shaking her head in disbelief at her admission. 'I think I've had too much to drink! You're not trying to take advantage of me, are you?'

'Perish the thought!' I laugh. 'The truth is, given I normally have to rely on my father to negotiate on my behalf, I find that getting women drunk is the only way I can persuade them to date me. But have no fear. I promise not to take advantage of you.'

'Oh yeah?' demands Carrie, her embarrassment swift to disappear. 'How can you be so confident? You don't fancy me, huh?'

'I'm not sure that statement could be any further from the truth,' I admit quietly. 'But it is getting late. So to ensure I'm not accused of taking advantage, I guess I should probably take you home?'

'I mean, that *is* a bit boring but I guess you should.'

'*Boring*?! I don't think I've ever been called that before!'

'Not to your face, perhaps,' she replies, before dissolving into laughter again. 'I do believe that teasing you might well become my all-time favourite hobby!'

'Is that right?' I enquire. 'I have a feeling it won't be long before I feel the same way about you.'

BY THE TIME we've strolled back to the car beneath a clear, moonlit sky, Carrie has sobered up and I want her more than ever. We chat amiably for the entire journey back to her house but that whole time, my fingers are itching to reach across and caress her. I discover that it takes all of my available willpower to fight those natural instincts.

'It's just here on the right,' she explains, as I pull up in front of a very pleasant, three-bedroom, semi-detached house in a quiet street. 'Nothing compared to your home, of course...'

'Please don't,' I urge, shaking my head lightly as I kill the engine. I would hate for Carrie to feel in any way inferior to me because of where we each live. I'm well aware that I won the genetic lottery, born into a life of wealth and privilege. I've pretty much been handed my entire life on a plate, whereas I don't doubt she's had to work hard for her living. Our two situations are incomparable and I respect her enormously for everything she's achieved.

Opening my door, I walk around to Carrie's side of the car to assist her out. As she takes my hand in hers, I stifle a small groan as my cock twinges in response to her soft touch. Really, she is *way* too tempting. As she rests against the car, I can sense myself naturally leaning in closer. I can smell her sweet perfume, feel the heat from her skin, her soft, fast breaths being dragged in and out of her lungs. My own breathing is equally noisy, mirroring what I assume is her desire.

Bending low, I drop a chaste kiss onto her cheek, just as she groans throatily, instantly confirming she wants more.

'It's too soon,' I moan, mindful that my cock is already standing to attention. I mustn't lean any closer, or she'll be made completely aware of my barely contained lust.

'Yes, it is,' she agrees, her hand unexpectedly reaching out to take hold around my waist. 'And let's not forget that you don't fancy me anyway.'

'Carrie,' I groan, as her hand pulls me closer. The moment my hardened length pushes against her pelvis, she groans again, this time long and deep. I lean my elbow against the car roof, our breath starting to ghost across each other's faces, mixing in our partially opened mouths. Every cell of my body is buzzing as an urgency engulfs me. An urgency to fuck this woman. To pleasure this woman. To love *this* woman. 'I promised not to take advantage of you tonight.'

Scooping up her arm, I lead Carrie to her front door, trying not to kick myself for making such a promise. But deep down, I know it's the right thing to do. She's had a few drinks and the last thing I want is for her to regret me. Maybe on Saturday we'll see things differently, but for now, the answer has to be no.

'Maybe *I* might take advantage of *you?*' she suggests, her mouth curving into the smile I've been growing increasingly fond of all day. 'Do you want to come in for a coffee?'

Oh God! Standing at her front door, I'm wondering how the hell I'm supposed to resist. Am I being tested in some way?

'No. Thank you,' I reply stiffly.

'It's just a coffee,' she teases.

'Yeah, but do you mean a coffee, or a *coffee?*' I grin. Flirting comes so easily with Carrie, I'm discovering that I just can't help myself.

'I mean a coffee,' she replies, looking confused. 'What's the difference?'

'If you don't know, I'm not going to be the one to tell you,' I laugh. 'But something tells me that you know.' The way she starts chewing on that damn lip of hers again confirms my assumptions are correct.

'Seriously, we shouldn't,' I say, trying to sound like I mean it. 'If we do any more than we already have, I won't be able to stop myself.' I can't hide the disappointment in my tone when I admit to this. 'As it is, I've had the nicest day. Even though it started off questionably, by being shouted at by a mad woman having a piss behind one of my trees. But it's got a lot better since then. Thank you.'

We both smile at each other warmly.

'No, thank you,' Carrie replies.

Picking up her hand, I kiss the back of it gently before sending her a cheeky wink.

'See, I stand by my promises,' I explain, feeling rather smug that I've succeeded. 'I promised not to seduce you, and here we are.'

'Seduction can be done in more than one way,' Carrie replies. 'You do know that, right?'

'Oh yeah?'

'Yeah. Not just through physical interaction.'

'In that case, I look forward to finding out much more about the subject on Saturday,' I tease, releasing her hand.

'As do I. Hey, Richard,' she mutters, lifting up onto tippy toes and giving me every indication that she wants to share a secret. Obligingly, I lower my ear towards her mouth.

'I'm so wet for you right now,' she whispers, her soft breath caressing my ear lobe. As my brain processes her wicked words, a low moan rumbles deep in my throat as animal instinct takes over. With those few simple words, Carrie has instantly proven her point that seduction can be undertaken by words, as well as touch. Does she seriously know how close to the edge she's pushing me? I'm already throbbing hard for her, the ache in my groin powerful and deep. Never before have I desired someone or something so completely. Particularly when that person is currently out of bounds. It's unbearable. Instinctively, my hands raise to her head. Pushing back her long locks from the side of her face, I expose her neck and ear, before placing my mouth against her soft, fragrant skin.

'And I'm gonna fuck you so hard for teasing me,' I mutter through gritted teeth, loving the sound of her breathy grunts that my words inspire. 'But I stand by my promises, so that's not happening tonight. Be ready for me on Saturday, though.'

And with that, I kiss and nip straight down her neck, only stopping when I reach her exposed collar bone. I feel Carrie's knees buckle, as the full weight of my sensuality briefly overwhelms her and she realises exactly what she's started with me. Good. I want her to be thinking about this for every minute until we meet again. Life's all about give and take. She's been giving all day. On Saturday, she'll learn how to take.

'Goodnight,' I say, releasing her body which is now slumped against the side of her house. I purposefully step back, in order to put some physical distance between us.

'Goodnight,' she attempts to reply, but all I hear are some disjointed sounds which make no sense.

For a little while we stand there, just gazing hungrily at each other.

'This is the part where you traditionally let yourself inside the house,' I tease, loving the fact that she's so overwhelmed by what we've shared. I can hardly blame her; every inch of my skin continues to tingle, while each beat of my heart is being mirrored by my aching cock.

'Yes...yes,' she agrees, managing to lever herself fully upright. Inhaling a deep breath, she steps up to the front door as elegantly as she can under the circumstances, taking an embarrassingly long time to get the key into the lock.

I consider helping her but, to be honest, if I touch her again I'll be lost. So instead, I very purposefully walk back to the driver's side of my car, leaning across the roof to observe her from afar. Eventually, she's successful and the front door swings open. Carrie glances back at me and raises her hand. I do the same, sending her an accompanying smile as she steps over the threshold and out of sight. Immediately, I glance at my watch. Fuck. How many hours until Saturday morning, and more to the point, can I seriously stay away from her for that long?

CHAPTER 7

CARRIE

I can't help it. The more time I spend with him, the more I realise I'm falling for him. Richard is quite simply the kindest, funniest, sexiest and most decent guy I think I've ever been lucky enough to meet, and our entire day together has been an absolute blast. From the first second he picked me up this morning, through our time working together to prepare Freddie for the race, I'm not sure we've stopped laughing. And now I'm very grateful that he refused to accept my original apology, instead seeing a potential between the two of us which I was blind to at first. A connection...the simple thrill of being in each other's company. But I can't deny I need more now. I want to be intimate with him. I tried...maybe not hard enough...on the night he dropped me back home, but now the desire burns within me like a furnace, overpowering every other emotion.

'Hey! Hey! Mrs!' Richard's raised voice drifts into my subconscious, interrupting my train of thought. Not breaking my stride beside Freddie, I glance around behind to see one smoking-hot, sexy man smiling warmly at me. He is perched up on Freddie's back, jockey-style, his knees pulled up high on the saddle. And despite the horse occasionally leaping around in excitement, Richard maintains incredible control of his steed, only ever using light, gentle hands on his horse's mouth. Shit! I feel a flutter of arousal daring to spread through me and try to suppress it. I should not be getting turned on by thinking about that but the truth is, I've been fantasising about those very hands exploring all over my body...and preferably inside me too.

'They're calling you!' he exclaims, pride leaching from his voice. 'Get on up there!'

'What?!' I exclaim, glancing around stupidly.

'You've just won the best turned out horse award...and you deserve it too! So hold your head up high and get your sexy bum onto that podium.'

Still unable to believe what's happening, I hear the commentator announcing Richard's name as the owner of the best turned out horse. And typical of the guy I'm quickly discovering him to be, refusing to take any credit for our work, he's insisting that I collect the prize. Smiling so hard that my cheeks are starting to ache, I stride up to the podium. It doesn't quite seem right that I'm being rewarded for succeeding in an activity I enjoyed so much. Applying all of my Pony Club tricks of the trade I thought I'd forgotten, I actually hadn't had quite so much fun in ages. The smell of the hoof oil as I painted it on, the feel of the horse's muscles contracting as I brushed him; it all gave me such a buzz. And if I do say so myself, Freddie does look pretty amazing. Although it obviously helps that the horse was in peak physical condition to start with. But I am rightly proud of our achievement, and I can see from Richard's face that he is too. Somehow, it is that realisation that means the most; I'm not sure why but I want him to be proud of me.

'You think my bum is sexy?' I enquire, trying but failing to look unamused, as I return back to Richard and Freddie afterwards.

'I think every single part of you is sexy,' Richard admits, shaking his head lightly. 'Now, wish me luck, and stop making me think about things which might force the blood to rush away from my brain or my heart.'

'But I might not want to wish you good luck,' I smirk, gazing straight up at him. 'Not when I've bet good money on *Georgie's Lot* to win.'

'You wouldn't dare!' he mutters, looking genuinely shocked.

'Wouldn't I just?'

'Not unless you want me to discipline you accordingly, the moment we get back to the horsebox! You do know that most women would promise me something at this point, to provide me with an incentive that makes winning worthwhile?'

'Well, I guess I'm not *most* women,' I shrug, as the other horses start to canter away, to head towards the starting line. Struggling to prevent his trusty steed from automatically following the rest of the pack, Richard quickly replies.

'You can say that again.'

'Good luck!' I shout, as they turn to join the rest of the competitors at considerable speed. Silently, I chastise myself as I watch him go. Another missed opportunity to be more assertive and let Richard know how much I desire him. After all, he's not exactly trying to hide the fact that he's attracted to me.

In all honesty, I feel incredibly nervous as I watch the race, hoping that neither Richard nor Freddie fall and hurt themselves. But my concerns are unwarranted. Riding like a man possessed, the two of them cruise around the track like a well-oiled machine, wiping the floor with the rest of the competition. I knew I'd been correct the very first time I saw Richard ride. He is a natural horseman. Intuitive, and with a powerful strong body that I increasingly fantasise about being wrapped around, he works with the horse, rather than against it. As a result, they easily outclass the competition. Indeed, mere seconds after the race has begun, I have no question in my mind who will win, barring an unexpected fall or accident. Richard's got it in the bag. Sure enough, minutes later he sails victorious past the winning post, his fist jubilantly punching the air as he sends me a cheeky wink.

The spectators roar with unconcealed delight. It's immediately very obvious that Richard is popular with the locals. Poor Freddie is being positively swamped with well-wishers offering congratulations, although given the horse is spending most of the time burrowing his nose into people's pockets in search of treats, he doesn't seem particularly fazed by the thronging crowds. Thrillingly, they head back in my direction and I swiftly realise that Richard only has eyes for me.

'Congratulations! You were amazing!' I say with obvious admiration, taking Freddie by the reins as we are directed towards the winner's enclosure. With an accompanying grin, Richard leans down towards me.

'Tell me I'm amazing later and I'll be even happier,' he admits gruffly.

Instantly, I feel a thud of desire hit me hard, right in the centre of my chest. And then my wishes become crystal clear. I want him. Ideally now, but certainly today. I wanted him almost as soon as we first met, but now my desire has grown stronger than ever.

'Me too,' I reply, enjoying the look of surprise on his face, just before he's directed to collect his prize winnings.

WITH BOTH OF us working as a team, in no time at all Freddie is untacked, washed down and happily installed inside the luxury lorry with water and hay to munch upon. During the entire time, Richard keeps his hands to himself. But just from his demeanour, I can tell that he's still riding an adrenaline high after winning and, if I'm not mistaken, feeling equally as horny as I am.

'Now,' he states in a no-nonsense tone. 'I do believe we've got a certain matter to resolve?'

'We have?' I ask, swallowing hard in response to his incredibly intense expression.

'We have,' he confirms. Taking hold of my hand he leads me gently but firmly into the living area of the horsebox. His thumb delicately strokes the inside of my wrist, undoubtedly as a ploy to turn me on, which I have to admit is working. I follow willingly, aware of him closing the door firmly behind us, once we're inside.

'Now, let's see this betting slip of yours for *Georgie's Lot*,' he demands, holding out his hand. He looks so serious and strict that I naturally bite down on my lip as my clit tingles involuntarily. Now I wish I really had put a bet on one of the competition, just to see what his reaction would be. With a smile, I pull a betting slip out of my pocket and hand it over to him, loving the broad grin that spreads across Richard's face, when he realises that I bet on him to win.

'Lucky,' he growls, taking one step closer. Naturally, I step backwards to continue gazing up at him, only to find myself leaning against the interior wall. Richard advances one more step and suddenly I'm trapped by his uber-sexy physique. But most frustratingly, although I'm encompassed by his delicious masculine scent and warmth, not a single point of our bodies touch.

'Tell me you don't want me,' he moans, his breath dancing through my hair, making my brain and body weak. 'Tell me you don't want me, right here, right now, and I'll walk away.'

'I don't...' I start to utter in a soft groan, but my words are cut short by his interruption.

'Liar.'

I swallow hard, closing my eyes against his overwhelming sexuality. Every part of me aches for him, so why am I being so bloody pigheaded, when he's apparently offering me what I want on a plate?

'You're a player,' I say, somewhat accusingly.

'That's unfair,' he replies. 'I'm playful, but not a player. I don't play with emotions. That's something only boys do. I grew out of that behaviour a long, long time ago. So, do you want me, or not?'

'Are you always this direct?' I ask, practically panting now. I can feel the heat rising from my cheeks and my eyes struggling to remain open, as I allow the wall of the horsebox to take the majority of my weight. Heat is flooding between my legs as I'm overcome with raw need. I'm not sure I've ever desired another human being so damn much in my life.

'Do you always answer every question with another question?' he smirks, his hand reaching out to gently caress the side of my ass, playfully teasing. Instantly, I emit a whimper which undoubtedly tells Richard everything he needs to know about my state of mind.

'Why? Do you?' I dare to retort, a small smile escaping my lips, purely because I enjoy the act of pushing him one step further. But the truth is, experiencing him this close up is overwhelming, not least because my skin is bristling with each and every one of his breaths that ghosts over me. I'm so stunned by his proximity that I'm pretty surprised I managed to speak those three words in the correct order.

'You're gonna cause me so much trouble,' he moans, leaning into me further. 'And I can't wait.'

I tremble lightly, able to feel his hardness pressing gently against me. The knowledge that he's as turned on as I am does bad things inside me. Feeling weak and willing, I know I'll be guided by whatever he wants because the truth is, I want to experience everything with this achingly sexy man.

Following a pause, Richard's hand tenderly captures my jaw and encourages my mouth towards his. With every hormone and feel-good chemical pumping through my bloodstream like some kind of hallucinogenic drug, I almost pass out from the high. With the gentlest imaginable caress, Richard's lips brush seductively across my own. Instantly, a low moan echoes up from both of our throats, confirming our joint desire for more. Much, much more. Entirely naturally, my hands wrap around his divine physique, pulling him closer, as his mouth returns, this time suckling gently on my lower lip. Convinced I feel the brush of his tongue at one point, I dig my finger-nails into his thighs as my lips part slightly, silently begging for more.

Fortunately, Richard takes the hint. Relentless with his affection, I am treated to a masterclass in kissing as our groans intensify and our tongues ultimately combine. I know I'm unbelievably wet at this point. I'm *so* damn ready for him. And still our kiss deepens further. Accompanied by a violent thrill of desire, I simply allow the sensations to overwhelm my body as I become lost in a kiss so sensual that it ought to be X-rated. Richard is proving himself to be everything I'd hoped, and a damn sight more besides. He's the person I've been failing to meet for my entire life, and right now, I literally want to drown in him.

CHAPTER 8

RICHARD

Carrie is so perfectly responsive. I love the way she reacts to every stroke of my fingers, every squeeze of my hand, or each minute flicker of my tongue. And she's turned on. I mean, I'm not surprised because I'm as hard as iron myself. But I can smell her arousal rising up between our warm bodies, and that knowledge alone is driving me onto greater endeavours, wanting to make this the very best experience for both of us. It takes a long, long time but eventually we part to draw breath, our chests expanding and contracting sharply as we stare into each other's lust-filled eyes; high on the intoxicating drug that is euphoria.

'I love it when I'm right,' I admit, sounding purposefully boastful. A small giggle escapes her lips.

'And what exactly do you believe yourself to be right about this time?' Carrie's eyes are sparkling, her cheeks flushed and a huge smile lighting up her face. She looks infinitely beautiful.

'That you'd kiss like an angel. And you do.'

'Is that right?' she smiles, her fingers still stroking temptingly around my lower back.

'I think so,' I reply, appreciating that my breathing has recovered enough to start all over again. 'Although, you've got a point. Perhaps I do just need another reminder. Just to be sure?' And with us both grinning like crazy idiots, our mouths combine once again, as we kiss with a growing sense of confidence and desire. It isn't until poor Freddie stomps on the floor of the horsebox in frustration that I realise we can't stay here forever, as much as we might both wish to. Unwillingly, I draw away.

'To be continued?' I suggest, attempting to straighten up my clothing. Although no matter how hard I try, a pair of skin-tight jodhpurs is never going to hide an erection of this size. I am throbbing for Carrie; every beat of my heart, every second of my existence. I currently have but one purpose. I fleetingly wonder if we couldn't just make love right now, in this room. After all, it has a small bed. Not very comfortable though.

'Definitely,' she confirms. 'But we must get Freddie home now.'

Her response ensures that sense prevails. No way is our first time going to be here in a horsebox. What the hell was I thinking? Ha! I know exactly what I was thinking – nothing. Because my cock was thinking for me.

As I drive the few miles back home, our flirty, sexy conversation continues, while our fingers continually intertwine.

'So, is this what you do then?' grins Carrie. I'm aware of her flashing me a smirk, even though my eyes are largely on the road ahead. 'Hunt down random women for a one-off shag and then dump them and move on? Is this behaviour why your father so despairs that you'll never settle down?'

'I hugely resent that implication!' I joke. 'For a start, *you* came onto *my* property and initiated conversation with *me*. If anything, you could be considered the instigator of this current scenario!'

'Then I'm extremely proud of myself,' Carrie laughs, only making me want her even more. But then she unexpectedly switches the course of the conversation entirely. 'What do we need to do for Freddie when we get back?'

'Check him over, feed him, and put him out in the field for a well-deserved rest. The tack will probably require a clean too...and the horsebox will need skipping out.'

'Wow, what did your last slave die of?' she bites back playfully.

'Satisfaction,' I admit, without missing a beat.

'You are so full of yourself!' she laughs. Just in time, I abandon my dirty retort that I'd prefer Carrie was full of me instead, and somehow manage to continue with our more appropriate conversation.

'Although when we get back to the stables, I was going to ask Jonathan to take over.'

'Jonathan?' she queries, as I pull into the front entrance of my property and drive towards the stable block.

'My groom,' I grin, knowing this admission is going to land me in a whole heap of trouble with Carrie; something I'm secretly looking forward to.

'Oh! So *now* you're going to use your groom!' she exclaims, reacting just as I'd anticipated.

'Well, I've already got what I want out of our little arrangement, haven't I?' I explain, sending her a cheeky glance to show that I'm only joking.

Alert as ever, I can see my groom already approaching from the back of the stables by the time I jump out of the lorry.

'Hey Jonathan!' I call out, while assisting Carrie down from her side of the high cab and ensuring I keep a firm hold of her hand afterwards. I'm certainly not afraid to show my affection for this incredible woman already. And I need her to know that.

'Good afternoon, Sir,' he responds. I perform a basic set of introductions, before adding my request for a favour. 'Would you mind doing the honours?'

'Of course not,' he replies, as we unfasten the back of the horsebox and pull down the ramp. Freddie is standing inside with an excessive amount of hay thrown onto the crown of his head. It makes him look endearingly like the customary village idiot. 'How did you get on?'

'We won,' I confirm. 'All of us,' I add with pride, nodding towards the Best Turned Out prize which Carrie is still clutching. She hasn't let it out of her sight since she was first presented with it; a fact that only endears me to her further.

'Wow! Great! Congratulations!'

With much more important things on my mind than exchanging pleasantries, I thank Jonathan and wind up our conversation.

'Follow me,' I murmur to Carrie, striding towards my home.

'What are you doing?'

'As if you don't know!' My reply is as straight-faced as I can manage. 'I'm inviting you in for a coffee, of course.' I'm not surprised when Carrie starts to giggle.

'Or if you'd prefer, I can upgrade that to *a coffee*?'

We both grin at each other and I see an increasingly familiar flush starting to pass across her face.

'I'd quite like a coffee, actually,' she confirms with a knowing smile.

'Yeah, I thought you might.' Dirty girl.

As we approach the front door, hand in hand, there is literally only one thing on my mind. Alas, my pleasurably carnal thoughts are interrupted by the unexpected appearance of my father.

'Hey kids!' he calls out, looking delighted at the sight in front of him. I squeeze Carrie's hand even tighter.

'Hi, Dad.'

'Good afternoon, Your Grace,' says Carrie, respectfully. Suppressing a grin, I have an urge to gather her up into my arms. I'll have to explain to her that, despite his title, my father is actually a very down-to-earth guy. Although to be fair, she couldn't be expected to know that, given this is only the second time they've met. Fortunately, Dad beats me to it.

'Call me Phillip. Please, my dear. I insist.'

'Thank you.'

'So, have you had a good day?'

'It's been amazing!' confirms Carrie, with considerable enthusiasm. Looking slightly confused, Dad looks between the two of us and then adds.

'And how did you do at the races? You were talking about the races I assume?'

'Er, yes, of course,' she stutters, making it blatantly obvious that she wasn't. If I had to guess, she was thinking about our exquisitely sensual kiss. Or should that be kisses?

'Liar,' I mouth in her direction, as my father glances away for a second. Instantly, her cheeks turn a slightly darker red. 'We won,' I confirm, acknowledging the team effort.

'Ah, well done my lad. You always said that horse would come right in the end, didn't you?' I nod, acknowledging he's quite correct. I have an eye for some things. Decent horses is one. I'm hoping that my perfect partner is another, because Carrie's certainly ticking a hell of a lot of boxes so far.

'Well, I'll catch up with you later, no doubt.' And with a final wave of his hand, he ambles away towards his car. With indecent haste, I tow Carrie inside, towards my private living quarters.

'You know the dinner and the concert we're due to go to?' she starts, slightly apprehensively.

'Ye-es?' I reply, failing to hide my spreading grin. I'm getting quite good at reading Carrie's thoughts already, and I'm hoping beyond hope that she's about to suggest what I've had on my mind all day.

'Do you think we should skip it?'

'But then you'll have worked for me, and not been paid in any way,' I respond, innocently.

'Perhaps you can find another way to reward me?' she suggests, attempting to sound equally innocent and failing completely.

'Perhaps I can.' I hear her inhale sharply, confirming that's exactly what she'd like to happen. 'But how do you suggest we keep ourselves occupied, if we aren't going to go out?'

'I have a few ideas,' she grins. Only a few? I have a few thousand, and once I get started, I'm not sure I'll be able to stop.

'But what about your Dad?' Carrie suddenly asks. 'He lives here too. He isn't going to walk in on us, is he? Is that why you're so hopeless at attracting women?' she adds as a most cheeky afterthought.

'Joking right up to the end, huh?' I enquire, enjoying watching her squirm slightly. I have to say, I do admire her spirit, even though I might have to gently punish her for suggesting I can't attract women. And I know exactly what form that punishment is likely to take too.

We reach the exterior entrance to my living quarters. Pushing the door open, I encourage Carrie to step inside first, before following on behind.

'This is my private area of the house,' I explain, locking the door firmly behind us and handing Carrie the key. 'Of which you are now in charge.'

'Mmmm, I like being in charge,' she admits, pocketing the key, before reaching out for my shirt and pulling me closer.

'Yeah, I guessed that,' I moan. 'Don't get used to it. And to answer your question about my father. He would only be permitted entry to this part of the house if you unlock the door. Although, I'm not sure what you've got to be concerned about. After all, what's the harm in him interrupting us having a coffee?'

CHAPTER 9

CARRIE

I love that Richard is playful but right now, I'm in no mood for games. I have a desire burning through me...a need, the like of which I've never known before. It's a powerful urge to feel him inside me, to be consumed by this amazing man. For us to become one. Instinctively, my hand leaves his waist and provocatively dares to descend. When my fingers brush lightly across the substantial bulge beneath his jodhpurs, he grunts with desire, causing my nipples to tighten in response.

'I want you. I just want you,' I admit, throatily. It feels as though there isn't a moment to waste.

With a knowing look, I grab Richard's hand and start to march him down the corridor. I literally have no idea where I'm heading but that doesn't stop me. My grand plan is to keep walking until I find something that looks vaguely like his bedroom. Unfortunately, I'm being presented with a damn sight more rooms than I'd been anticipating. Ordinarily, I'd be amazed at the beauty of his enormous home, hung with what look to be original oil paintings and draped with silks and other fine fabrics. But right now, being a woman on a mission, the furnishings are scarcely being permitted a second glance.

'Try this door on the left,' Richard suggests beside me, sounding pleased with himself. Actually, he's sounding a lot more than pleased. I might go so far as to describe his tone as gleeful. Not that I mind, given that's exactly how I feel too.

The instant we stumble through the doorway, it's obvious that Richard has led me to his bedroom. An enormous four-poster bed dominates the exquisite space, with views across an attractive, private garden. Feeling so horny that it's making me unusually courageous, I push Richard gently back onto the bed into a sitting position, before commencing a slow, seductive strip, for his eyes only.

'Oh baby,' he groans, both his eyes and mouth open wide as he hungrily devours my performance. 'Mmmm, go on. Good girl.' Buoyed by his blatant desire, it isn't long before I'm swaying in front of him, wearing only my black lace underwear and a large smile.

'Here, let me,' he offers. His hands reach temptingly out for me, fingers rotating over my hips in a way that makes continuing to stand upright a significant challenge. As he strokes my bra straps down my arms, sighing deeply as he exposes my aching nipples, I'm forced to question how sensible the decision to provide a strip tease actually was. Leaning closer, his soft, moist lips begin to kiss daringly around my tummy and lower. And when his fingers loop beneath the waistband of my panties, temptingly zig-zagging the final item of clothing down my thighs and away, I realise that my legs have physically started to shake. It's all very well being sexually assertive, but maybe this wasn't my best ever idea; certainly not in the presence of such an overwhelmingly sexy and seductive man. Fortunately, Richard recognises the dangers, easing me down onto the bed, before standing up himself.

'Are you sure about this?' he enquires gently, shrugging off his shirt without embarrassment. And quite rightly too; his body is divinely sculpted and causes my fingertips to start tingling, such is my urgency to explore.

'Absolutely,' I reply, practically panting.

He nods almost imperceptibly, before turning his attention to the rest of his clothing, which is pushed down and away in one fell swoop. Instantly, the breath catches in my throat as my entire abdomen clenches hard. Fully erect and as hard as iron, Richard is not a small guy. I very soon discover that he is, however, an extremely tender lover.

Crawling onto the bed, he gently eases me into a horizontal position before folding his incredible physique above me. The sensation of our skin sliding together for the first time causes the kind of high which could make a girl faint with pleasure. I groan with satisfaction; a sound instantly mirrored by Richard. This feels so damn right and we both know it. We just fit together, mentally and physically. Seconds later, our mouths join back together as our hands start to explore. Instantly, it feels as though a catch has been released, and our true desires can now be allowed to grow and blossom. Grinding against him I can feel his thickened length, hard and ready, as Richard touches me, without ever really *touching* me. All he seems willing to offer is a hugely frustrating tease, which I can only bear for the shortest time.

'I need you inside me,' I instruct. If I sound desperate, it's because I am. And although it's out of character for me to be quite this demanding, I'm way past caring.

'No deal,' he grunts. 'Besides, I have some payback to administer first.'

'P...payback?' I stutter, my mind suddenly becoming very fuzzy, as a slow, heavy throb commences deep down.

'Mmmmm,' he confirms, unexpectedly scraping his teeth down my neck. His actions instantly send a surge of goosebumps up my spine and into the base of my skull. Without pausing, Richard starts to kiss tenderly across my collar bone, before heading south. I'm ridiculously aware of my hardened nipples, standing to attention as they eagerly await his ministrations. Right now, I want nothing more than for him to suck them into his talented mouth and make me feel alive. But that glorious moment doesn't arrive. Instead he hovers over my throbbing flesh, continually causing me to whimper.

'What have I done to deserve payback?' I eventually manage to stutter.

'General sassiness,' he confirms, before blowing a narrow stream of cool breath across my exposed nubs, instantly causing them to harden further. He immediately follows this up with his warm tongue and I shout out my pleasure and surprise into the ancient room.

'Delicious,' groans Richard, before repeating the same with my other nipple.

Mindful how wet my throbbing pussy is, I daringly open my legs and wrap them around Richard's powerful form, insistently pulling him closer.

'I want you.' My voice is low, urgent and entirely truthful.

'I know,' he whispers, allowing his teeth to intermittently graze against my nipple, simply to discover how intense my reactions will be. 'I want you too, but all in good time.'

With a low moan, I roll my pelvis against him feeling ravenous. His attitude is frustrating, intriguing but incredibly erotic and only makes me want him more. I've had partners before who would buckle under my demands, but apparently not this one. I open my mouth to challenge him again, but my words are interrupted by the thrilling knowledge that he's starting to descend further down my body. With a moan of pre-emptive bliss, I arch my spine away from the bed, eager to feel the kind of ecstasy that Richard is ready to provide. But instead, I find myself increasingly denied.

I cry out when his mouth dares to rake up and down my inner thighs, which are now splayed wide open in anticipation. His breath occasionally ghosts near my clit, and I'm convinced I feel the lightest brush of one fingertip against my swollen, needy flesh. Just once. Maybe. As a consequence, I'm a mass of writhing desire, leaping at the merest suggestion of his attentions, as I twist beneath his purposefully torturous presence. I have never felt so swollen, wet or ready for anyone. The sensation is nothing short of bewitching.

'Richard,' I implore, sounding like a woman on the very edge of her sanity. 'Please. Don't make me wait.'

'I never hid the fact that I'd enjoy treating you in this way,' he murmurs, before inhaling with obvious enjoyment. 'You were given fair warning. When you said that teasing me was becoming your all-time favourite hobby, I agreed I felt the same way.'

'But I didn't mean this kind of teasing!' I gasp as his hands slide beneath my ass, lifting me into a better position for whatever wickedness I don't doubt he has planned. With my hips raised higher, my legs automatically fall open wider, like I wasn't exposed enough.

'Well, I did. You should learn to be more specific.'

And with that, his hands begin to gently massage my deep-set muscles, each movement somehow stretching my pussy open wider for him.

'Oh God,' I groan. This is too much. I can't bear this level of anticipation. I had no idea Richard was going to be like this. He is overwhelming me in every possible way and, what's worse, I love it. 'Pleeeeeeeease,' I almost sob.

I guess he must recognise the agonising need in my tone because seconds later, his tongue sweeps through my swollen, sodden lips, fleetingly parting them in order to scoop up a sample of nectar. My reaction is immediate and extreme, convulsing against the bed as all conscious thought leaves me. I'm on a higher plane of existence right now, with no plans to descend back down to the mortal world until I'm absolutely forced to do so. As it flickers, swoops and probes, I'm very quickly discovering that Richard's tongue is a thing of wonder. And I am one hell of a lucky woman. Within no time, he has me balanced on the very edge of orgasm but, like before, he seems intent on making me wait. And no matter how much I pant, moan and grind myself against him, the man won't be persuaded.

By the time he eventually retracts, I'm in an unenviable state. Having been held on the edge for so long, I can't think, I can't focus, I can barely move and I sure as hell can't stop shaking. From a place far away, I'm vaguely aware of him tearing open a condom wrapper; an action which has the effect of slightly sobering me up from my daze of sexual intoxication. I've been so overwhelmed that I'm ashamed to admit I hadn't even considered contraception. And here Richard is, looking after me, without even questioning it.

'I want this to last a long time,' he admits, his voice little more than a growl. 'But I fear that's not going to happen. Not once I'm inside of you. You...do things to me.'

A massive smile spreads across my face. Now I *very* much like the sound of that.

'So can we agree up front that this is one of...I don't know...several unions tonight?'

'Unions?' I query, a giggle already escaping from me.

'I was trying to find a nice way of saying "one of several times I'm going to fuck you senseless", and that was the best I could come up with,' he admits, raising an eyebrow in the form of a challenge. 'Next time, I'll just be direct.'

I attempt to sigh and shake my head, in order to suggest I'm far from impressed. The guy's already proving himself to be insatiable; a trait I greatly applaud. Unfortunately, the effect is spoiled by the huge shuddering groan I emit, as Richard smears his sheathed cock straight through the centre of my exposed lips.

'First of all, you were going to take me out to dinner and a rock concert,' I protest playfully, in between short, sharp gasps. 'Then we were going to enjoy this glorious encounter together. And now, all you're offering is a quick, unsatisfactory shag?'

'Yeah...I guarantee it won't be unsatisfactory, and it won't be that quick either,' he corrects. 'Just quicker than I want it to be. Although, given I have an urge to make love to you all weekend, that probably isn't saying very much.'

'I'm seriously contemplating asking to be paid in cash for all my hard work in the future, given I seem to have been a victim of false advertising.'

'I'll give you fucking false advertising!' he groans, nudging his stubbly jaw against my breast, as he lines himself up into the optimal position. 'You see what I mean about your general sassiness?'

'It's just the way I am,' I mutter, rolling my eyes back as he places the smallest amount of pressure behind his hips, allowing just the tip of his cock to slide inside me. 'Oh fuck!' I gasp.

'I love it,' he admits, sounding similarly affected. 'Never, ever change.'

And with that, he gently encourages our bodies closer together as he slides inside me for the very first time. It's a slow, continual but bliss-filled stretch I experience, which makes me gasp and curse at regular intervals, as he continues to sink his thick girth relentlessly inside.

'God, I am the luckiest man,' he sighs, seconds after he eventually bottoms out with a groan, filling me to absolute perfection. As it happens, he's not alone in thinking that; I truly feel like the most blessed woman alive. Unfortunately, that isn't something I can voice right now. I'm in no fit state to remember my name, far less string a sentence together. But something tells me I'll have plenty of opportunity to remind Richard of how amazing he makes me feel in the future. Hopefully for a very long time to come.

CHAPTER 10

RICHARD

I was mistaken when I believed Carrie merely kissed like an angel; it turns out she is an *actual* angel, sent down to earth for me. Everything I could ever dream of in a partner, she's funny, sassy, loving and kind. She's also tight, wet, and ready to climax, over and over again. And as I've discovered in the past hour, she has a body to die for. I want to worship each curve, using every inch of her delectable form to encourage the orgasms to flow. I have purposefully been holding her on the edge, ever since we entered the bedroom. But I don't doubt the number of peaks I could have helped her to ascend, had I been so inclined. Perhaps next time, she'll learn not to be quite so sassy, although secretly, I hope not. I don't want to change a single thing about her.

And far from freaking me out as this knowledge might have done in the past, I find it electrifying. Instinctively I know this is the woman I'll be happy to cherish forever, if she feels the same way. Sex has always been just sex to me, but already I can sense that isn't what we're sharing. There is a much deeper meaning behind every kiss, every movement, every touch. And although part of me is terrified, there's a larger part of me that's thrilled. At last, I'm tasting what a real partnership could be like.

'You've been riding all day,' breathes Carrie, drawing my focus back to the here and now. 'Perhaps it's my turn?'

I can't help smiling as I reposition onto my back and she straddles my hips. She's about as subtle as an erupting volcano. You see the thing is, I still haven't permitted her to come and I know it's driving her wild. I'm guessing she thinks she's got a better chance of taking control in this position. Unfortunately, as she sinks down onto my throbbing cock, I have to concede she might have a point. Instantly, I'm overwhelmed by the sight before me and my hands automatically reach out to caress her perfectly-shaped breasts.

As she moves, I can feel her clamping down hard, making me fear an early loss of control. The pressure and sensation very quickly become too much.

'Carrie, seriously,' I groan, my hands naturally fastening around her hips, in an attempt to take back some element of control. 'I need you to slow down.'

'Like this?' she asks, flashing me the cheekiest grin I've ever seen. Purposefully, she picks up the most wicked rhythm, practically guaranteed to make me lose it. *Fuck.* I have to retaliate. Pulling her pelvis down hard against me, I force our flesh to mesh together more firmly, smearing her clit against my groin.

'No, not like that. Like this.'

'Oh my God!' she gasps. My actions have the desired effect. It isn't long before her rhythm starts to falter, with the approach of her inevitable release. I wait for as long as I think I can get away with, before unexpectedly grabbing hold of Carrie and flipping her face-up. She growls with frustration, sounding more animal-like than ever. For what probably feels like the millionth time, her orgasm has been denied.

'I need to come,' she sobs. 'Fucking well let me come.'

'Then come for me. Hard,' I order. And, starting to drive my hips at pace, I commence a rhythm ultimately guaranteed to destroy both of us. But she's gonna come first. As far as we are concerned, she will always come first. In everything. Strangely, with this at the forefront of my mind, a degree of self-control returns. I can do this.

Within no time, Carrie's frantic moans begin to fill my bedroom. She's so tight I can hardly bear it, but somehow, as she starts to pulse and spasm around my cock, I manage to hold on. And then, like the inevitable crescendo of some great piece of classical music, her cries explode loudly throughout the room, echoing around the ancient fixtures and driving me on. I'm pretty confident this house hasn't witnessed so much excitement in decades, possibly centuries, and I for one am very keen to reverse that trend.

Somehow, I manage to fight my urge to come, subconsciously recognising the intense pleasure that I can give this incredible woman if I can just hold on a little longer. Carrie is already dissolving into her next climax, and then the next, as she starts to ride an overwhelmingly formidable orgasmic wave that I have no desire to assist her down from. Indeed, the more I rock myself deep inside, the louder she seems to become. Realising I never want this to end, I somehow manage to battle my own desires, in order that she can enjoy hers.

Eventually, shaking all over, Carrie visibly crumples beneath me, completely spent. Or, at least, that's what I suspect until I hear her highly suggestive request.

'I want you to go behind me.'

'Turn over, then,' I grin, before pulling out gently. To be honest, I'm pretty impressed I've managed to hold it together, but it feels like my turn now. With a groan of exhaustion laced with intense sexual desire, Carrie attempts to coordinate her limbs. It takes a little while, but she's eventually in a great position, with her head against the pillow and her ass high in the air.

'Wider,' I demand, nudging her thighs slightly further apart with my knee. Carrie responds with a hoarse moan. A sound that only grows more extreme when I duck my head down and allow my tongue to explore her swollen, well-pounded lips before flicking over her ass.

'Fuck!' she shrieks, suddenly wide awake.

'Dirty girl,' I chastise playfully, before landing my hand across her exposed ass cheek, watching her open her legs even wider to provide me with better access. 'You like that, huh?' I only receive a moan in response, but it's a piece of information I very happily file away for future reference.

'You know what dirty girls get, don't you?' I ask, carefully sinking back inside, the change of position making the entire experience feel more intense than ever.

'No,' she pants, her legs already visibly trembling. 'What do they get?'

'Everything they want. Although this particularly dirty girl should be prepared for the fact that I won't last long now. Just a warning.' It already feels *way* too intense and I'm not even fully inside her yet.

'That's what you said last time,' she replies, half chuckling, half groaning, as I fall back into a slow, determined rhythm which she mirrors.

But this time, I mean it. In an ideal world, perhaps I could last for ages but the truth is, I just need us both to enjoy ourselves and I'll be happy. There is something about this woman. She seems able to make me lose control of my feelings, of my body, of my senses. And the strange thing is, I don't care anymore. I want her so badly, I will do just about anything she asks. Particularly when what she asks is such a very enchanting proposition.

'Fuck me,' she begs. 'Harder.'

I'm not sure if Carrie sensed me holding back, but her words have broken any restraint I might have been displaying. Like a man possessed, I slam myself deep as she tightens around me, the tell-tale signals of her oncoming orgasm obvious. Her cries grow in volume and are swiftly combined with my own low moans, as my brain becomes fuzzy and my balls tighten further.

'Go on,' she gasps, aware of my hips taking on a life of their own. Seconds later, I am rocked by the insane intensity of my climax, as rope after rope of come jets deep within, the force of my guttural roar surprising even myself. Exhausted, we both collapse down onto the mattress and I carefully pull out.

'Fuck,' I eventually grunt, once my lungs have recovered enough to talk. 'That was...wow.'

'Yeah,' gasps Carrie in astonishment. 'Wow.'

Pulling her into my embrace, I hold her tightly, loving the feeling of being so close.

'That was the most amazing, satisfying, astonishing...' started Carrie, before turning to face me with a grin. 'If that's you not lasting very long, then I might be in trouble.'

'You *are* in trouble,' I confirm. 'I already want you again. Something I intend to rectify later tonight.'

'I knew it...insatiable,' she tuts.

'Are you hungry?' I'm well aware that Carrie hasn't eaten since lunchtime and I can't deny that she's used up considerable energy since then.

'For you, yes. Definitely,' she smiles.

'I'm serious. Are you up for going out?'

'As long as I don't have to walk very far!'

I glance at the alarm clock on the bedside table to check the time. Seeing a stack of tickets and invitations balanced there, I hand them over to Carrie.

'I feel bad about missing the concert today, when I know you were excited about going,' I explain. 'But I've got a load of VIP tickets and backstage passes for future events. I'll take you to one or all of them to make up for it, if you like?'

'How come you've got all of these?' she enquires, eyes open wide in amazement. I can understand her surprise; the set includes entry into hospitality boxes at huge sporting events, rock concerts, film premieres, and even a champagne balloon flight, to name a few.

'I'm a board member on a couple of influential projects,' I explain. 'It kind of comes as part of the deal.'

'And you don't use them?'

'I've never had anybody I want to go with before,' I explain with a small smile. 'But that's changed now. If you're amenable, I intend to start making use of these tickets straight away.'

'I'm definitely amenable! I'm highly amenable!' she giggles.

'I can vouch for that!' I laugh, feeling ridiculously lighthearted. 'So you'll accompany me?'

'Accompany you?' she exclaims. 'You're literally going to have to tie me down in order to stop me.'

'Tie you down, huh?' I enquire, immediately shifting the entire tone of our conversation. 'That is an extremely tempting offer, and a challenge I'm most happy to accept.'

'Richard!' Carrie murmurs, looking genuinely shocked.

Good. I'd hate her to think I was destined to be boring in any way.

'Sorry if you're disappointed, but this is me.'

'Trust me, I'm far from disappointed!'

With a smile, I kiss her again, slow and deep. By the time we pull apart, invitations are scattered all over the floor and a certain part of my anatomy is already starting to recover from our earlier workout. I glance at the clock again; it's nearly half past seven.

'Screw it!' I exclaim, feeling younger and more alive than I have in years. 'Let's cash in every one of these invitations *and* go to the concert tonight as well! We can grab something to eat there.'

'But the concert starts in less than ten minutes,' she argues, screwing up her face in confusion. 'Or have you also miraculously invented a time-machine while I've been enjoying the best sex of my life?'

The best sex of her life? Now, I like the sound of that! I try to suppress my delight by keeping my face expressionless, but I can't prevent my chest from swelling a little.

'So we'll miss the warm-up act,' I shrug.

'But it must be thirty miles away!' Clearly Carrie isn't going to let this rest, so I pick up the telephone and dial a number.

'Tommy? Yeah, if you don't mind please,' I confirm, aware that Carrie's only hearing one side of our conversation. 'Fifteen minutes would be great. Ta.' Feeling incredibly smug, I hang up.

'Who was that?' she demands, looking so serious that I have an urge to kiss her all over again. Followed by a lot more besides...but that will have to wait for a few hours. We have a concert to enjoy first.

'Helicopter pilot,' I admit. 'We're leaving in ten, so I suggest you go and get yourself ready!'

'Helicopter what? Oh, come on!' she complains, as I laugh at her disbelieving face. 'That's just showing off!'

EPILOGUE

RICHARD

1 **year later**
Desperately trying to control my fast, shallow breaths, I take a little more weight upon my arms to prevent squashing Carrie, as I gently pull out. She gazes up at me with those bright blue eyes, her long blonde curls spread across the pillow, looking infinitely beautiful. I still have to pinch myself every day. I really am the luckiest man to be able to call this astonishing woman my girlfriend, and go to bed with her every single night.

I'm addicted to the look of total satisfaction her expression is currently portraying. Since that first evening we spent together in my bed, I've relished finding out all about her wants, needs and desires, in the hope that I can fulfil her every fantasy. When she stares at me in this way, which seems to be happening with increasing regularity, I know I'm succeeding. And it's the best feeling in the world.

'I love you,' Carrie murmurs, running a hand tenderly across my cheek. Okay, maybe hearing those three words is the best feeling in the world. It's a close call.

'I love you too, baby.'

With a deeply contented sigh, I gather her into my arms. As we slowly start to fall asleep, my mind wanders. Ever since we first met,

Carrie has completely changed my life for the better. Long gone are Dad's hopeless attempts at setting me up, not least because he can see that I'm a ridiculously happy man who is very deeply in love. Of course, there are still a stack of invites and VIP tickets beside my bedside clock, but now Carrie and I take advantage of every single opportunity. Spending time with her is a blast and we are both committed to living our lives to the absolute full. It's difficult to believe that a spot of random badger watching, coupled with Carrie's urgent requirement to track down our non-existent woodland-based toilet facilities, would lead us to this point now. But I can't deny...I'm ecstatic they did.

For some reason, just as sleep threatens to engulf me, my thoughts drift towards Carrie and Dad. I saw them sitting outside in the shade earlier this afternoon, drinking white wine and sharing whatever scandalous gossip they'd most recently heard. Their relationship is joyous to observe and Dad undoubtedly adores Carrie. I do believe, in fact, that her presence has somehow brought us closer than we have been in years; yet another benefit of having such a wonderful woman in my life.

Almost asleep, I drop a soft kiss on the top of a sleeping Carrie's head as an adrenaline-filled bubble of excitement dares to explode within. Barely able to contain the thrilling sensation inside me, I start to grow increasingly more awake again. It won't be today, it won't be tomorrow, but one day soon I've got a big question to ask her. A question that I hope will make both me and Carrie, and to be honest my family too, beyond happy. Of course, it does depend on my strong-willed, independent, glorious woman answering the way I hope she will. But it's a question I will never apologise for asking, over and over again if I have to, because I know one thing for certain; Carrie is the person I've been waiting for my entire life. And I've got more than a sneaking suspicion that she feels exactly the same way about me too.

THE END

YOUR HELP PLEASE

T hank you for reading this book. I really appreciate your interest and support.

I am a self-published author who is trying to make my way in what is an incredibly competitive marketplace. One of the few ways I can compete against the big publishing companies is by getting multiple reads, ratings and reviews, as these gradually increase the exposure of my work.

Therefore, if you have enjoyed this book and would like to see me continue writing in the future, I would hugely appreciate it if you would please consider leaving a rating or review. This not only helps me to attract new readers and share my stories more widely, but any kind comments do genuinely provide me with the inspiration to keep writing.

Thank you so much.

Fenella

PATIENTS IS A VIRTUE

Need inspiration on what to read next? 'Patients is a Virtue', also by Fenella Ashworth, is a slow burn, steamy romance available from Amazon.

EVERY DAY OF HER LIFE, Olivia Jones conceals a secret that nobody else knows.

It wasn't planned. It's certainly not her choice. But thanks to a tedious mental block she hasn't been able to get past, at thirty years old, she's still a virgin. Fortunately, as a successful sex therapist, issues of this kind are Doctor Ben Wilson's forte.

Working closely with the painfully shy Olivia, the handsome Doctor gradually helps conquer the fears which have been holding her back for so long. In so doing, they uncover a playful, sensual, increasingly sexually self-confident woman, as well as their own developing, mutual attraction. An attraction they are forced to fight, for reasons of moral propriety and General Medical Council rules. But in the end, is all resistance futile?

Can the head be forced to overrule the heart, or will white-hot lust always ultimately triumph?

ABOUT THE AUTHOR

F enella is the author of many a steamy romance, in which she aims to provide scorching hot reads for the enjoyment of her awesome readers.

She lives in the South of England where her time is divided equally between looking after her family, drinking wine, thinking smutty thoughts, turning the aforementioned smutty thoughts into stories, and (possibly most importantly of all), avoiding doing any housework.

Much of Fenella's inspiration appears during peaceful, early morning walks with her mentally deranged Spaniel. Consequently, she spends her time bumbling around the countryside with her head buried in a notepad, falling into rabbit holes as she remains completely oblivious to the most spectacular sunrises.

Please show your support for this author by leaving reviews for her stories. This will enable her to find new readers and keep writing.

www.fenellaashworth.com

Printed in Great Britain
by Amazon

84902943R00127